NIGHTMARE HALL

THE SILENT SCREAM
THE ROOMMATE
DEADLY ATTRACTION
THE WISH
THE SCREAM TEAM
GUILTY
PRETTY PLEASE
THE EXPERIMENT

The Night Walker

As if in a trance . . .

The couple sat in a small car behind the tall, ivy-covered dorm.

It had just begun to rain, lightly at first, then more steadily. The windshield and windows were instantly covered with a thin sheen of wetness, as if they were sweating profusely. Later, the couple would say the rain was what kept them from seeing their attacker.

The figure moved slowly, deliberately, as if in a trance. It was shielded from the rain by a coat and hat. When it reached the small car, the right arm moved up, raising an object high above its head.

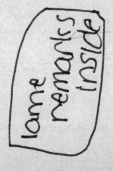
lame remarks inside

Terrifying thrillers by Diane Hoh:

Funhouse

The Accident

The Invitation

The Train

The Fever

Nightmare Hall: The Silent Scream

Nightmare Hall: The Roommate

Nightmare Hall: Deadly Attraction

Nightmare Hall: The Wish

Nightmare Hall: The Scream Team

Nightmare Hall: Guilty

Nightmare Hall: Pretty Please

Nightmare Hall: The Experiment

Nightmare Hall: The Night Walker

NIGHTMARE HALL

The Night Walker

DIANE HOH

SCHOLASTIC INC.
New York Toronto London Auckland Sydney

No part of this publication may be reproduced in whole or in part, or stored in a retrieval system, or transmitted in any form or by any means, electronic, mechanical, photocopying, recording, or otherwise, without written permission of the publisher. For information regarding permission, write to Scholastic Inc., 555 Broadway, New York, NY 10012.

ISBN 0-590-47688-2

12 11 10 9 8 7 6 5 4 3 2 1   4 5 6 7 8 9/9

Printed in the U.S.A.   01

First Scholastic printing, March 1994

NIGHTMARE HALL

The Night Walker

Prologue

Darkness. A thick curtain of soft velvety black.

Quinn Hadley stood in the door of her dorm room, arms outstretched in front of her. Her eyes were wide open. But they saw nothing.

She took one small cautious step, then another, her eyes gazing blankly out into the hallway.

Cold. Piercing cold.

Quinn shivered, clutching her thin nightgown around her.

The wandering had happened before. But she never knew . . . not until it was too late.

Silence. Not a sound.

But soon the screaming would begin.

Quinn's roommate awakened just in time to see Quinn head off down the hallway.

As if on a mission.

A deadly mission.

Chapter 1

Suddenly, there was a hand on Quinn Hadley's left arm, its cool fingers encircling her wrist. A familiar voice said with a hint of irritation, "Oh, Quinn, not again! How am I supposed to get any sleep if I have to hunt down my roommate in the middle of the night? I've got a heavy-duty psych exam tomorrow morning at eight. At *eight*, Quinn!"

Quinn, her dark brown eyes open but glazed, turned to face the voice. But she really didn't *see* the small, thin girl with very short ginger-colored hair and sleep-swollen green eyes. "I was *asleep*, Quinn! The way you should be. Well, I guess you still are, in a way. I know I'm not supposed to wake you up, so come on," she said, beginning to lead Quinn down the darkened hallway on the sixth floor in Devereaux dorm at Salem University. "Can we please go back to bed now?"

They padded quietly down the hallway, a tiny girl in a white T-shirt leading a tall, slender, silent figure who moved mechanically, robotlike. Because the girl named Quinn didn't argue or make any noise, no doors opened, no curious heads peered out to see what was going on.

"I specifically asked for a nonsmoking roommate," the small girl grumbled as she reached out to turn a doorknob. "It never occurred to me to request a nonsleepwalker! Who'd think of something like that?"

The door opened. Quinn was led inside and deposited firmly on one of a pair of long, narrow beds set against opposite walls. "Now, *stay* there," Quinn was told. "Please! I need my rest."

Quinn obediently lay down on the bed, curling her freezing feet tightly inside the blankets to warm them.

"This can't keep up," the voice continued, as bedsprings creaked across the room. "I get so cranky when I don't get enough sleep. The worst part is, you probably won't even remember this in the morning. . . ." The voice trailed off and became deep, even breathing. Asleep.

Quinn lay very still on her bed, her eyes closed. She was completely awake now. The sound of the door closing behind them had snapped her back to reality. The voice, she knew, belonged to Tobie Thomason, her roommate in room 602. She knew, too, although she hated to admit it, that Tobie had just rescued her from a sleepwalking episode.

Quinn tingled with shame. A college freshman, sleepwalking! Just like when she was a little kid in footed pajamas, wandering around in the dark looking for . . . for what? She'd never figured that out. Looking for her parents? For safety? No, her room had always felt perfectly safe. She'd never been afraid of the dark.

Her parents had never come up with an answer, either. When the problem worsened in Quinn's adolescence, her slightly embarrassed mother had taken her to a psychiatrist.

"Stress," he had announced firmly. "Alleviate the girl's stress and the problem will end."

And her mother had responded heatedly, "She's a *teenager*, doctor. Her entire *life* is stressful. Should we lock her in her room until she's twenty-one?"

Quinn had smiled, but the doctor hadn't. "No," he had said seriously, "that would be too drastic. However, it might be prudent to try locking her bedroom door at night. Just, of course, until she's over this crisis."

Her first visit with the good doctor had been the last.

Her parents *had*, though, locked her bedroom door, after installing a very expensive smoke alarm.

Several months later, the episodes had ended, for no apparent reason, just as they'd begun.

There had been a second siege shortly after her fifteenth birthday, and a third when she was sixteen. Each time, her parents had begun locking her bedroom door again until the episodes abruptly ended.

There had been no more since she was sixteen.

So it had been a terrible shock when Tobie had told Quinn about the first incident at Salem.

It was back at the beginning of the year. Orientation was behind them and their room had achieved some semblance of order. Their personalities were very different. Quinn was almost hyperactive, always on the move. If she was sitting still, her fingers were busy doodling or fidgeting with a paper clip or a pen or, in a restaurant, the salt and pepper shakers. Tobie was quieter and had a lot less energy. She often took naps after classes, and many evenings she was "too tired" to go out. The running joke in the dorm was that the two were "The Odd Couple" because Quinn, who needed to be occupied at all times, was a neat freak, and Tobie was the complete opposite.

"You're a dropper," Quinn had joked when they'd been in the room less than a week. "You come in and drop your books on your bed, you take your clothes off and drop them on the floor, and you drop your wet towels on the tile in the bathroom. My mother calls that a dropper."

Tobie's excuse was that it took too much energy to put things away.

But because Quinn appreciated having a calmer, quieter roommate to offset her own restless energy, and because Tobie liked the idea of having someone else keep things reasonably neat, they had settled into their new routine without too much effort.

Until Tobie told Quinn, one brisk September morning, "You were walking in your sleep last night."

Quinn had stared at her, awash with dismay.

"I woke up and your bed was empty," Tobie explained hesitantly, aware of Quinn's embarrassment. "At first, I thought you were in the bathroom. But when you didn't come back, I went hunting for you. You were just about to go down the fire stairs when I spotted you. You'd already opened the door. *That* really scared me. That stairway is dark. You could have fallen."

Quinn had had such a hard time dealing with this new episode, she'd talked to one of the school counselors. He, too, had mentioned "stress," but had been more understanding than the first doctor. "I know it's hard, now that you're at college. So much to do. But you must try to get plenty of sleep, don't wear yourself out studying or partying, and try some deep breathing exercises to help you relax before you go to sleep."

The advice was sound, and had seemed to be working.

So it was a bitter disappointment to realize that she had once again been prowling around the halls in her sleep.

Tears of frustration stabbed at Quinn's eyelids. There was no way in the world to keep every ounce of stress out of her life. That wasn't possible, not for anyone. Unless you lived in a bubble. This business with Simon, was that what had triggered this latest episode? She'd taken a nocturnal walk in the cold darkness because Simon Kent had suddenly and without explanation lost all interest in her?

No. No! That couldn't be what it was! She refused to believe that anyone had that kind of power over her. Not even someone as terrific as Simon had *seemed* to be.

It had to be something else. Maybe it was her killer calculus class. Maybe she was homesick. It could be anything. It *wasn't* Simon Kent.

Forcing herself to breathe deeply, Quinn pushed from her mind the nasty shock of finding herself sleepwalking again. Sleep . . . she needed sleep.

She needed sleep because this weekend was Spring Fling. A very big deal at Salem University. There were parties, bands, and activities out on the Commons, and the big formal dance . . .

She wasn't going to the dance. Not now.

But she'd be going to all of the other events, and she didn't want to be too tired.

Quinn rolled over on her side, wondering if Tobie would request a different roommate now. Her last thought before she finally fell into a deep sleep was, I don't want another roommate. She's not exactly Miss Excitement and she's as sloppy as a two-year-old, but I don't want to start all over again with someone new.

Quinn fell asleep envisioning a long line of new roommates, all of them staying in 602 only a night or two before packing their bags and jumping ship. Who wants to room with someone who haunts the halls at night like a vampire?

Quinn saw Simon twice the following Friday on the Commons. Both times, he hurried past her, his thin shoulders bent, his eyes on the ground as if he expected to find something of value there. But she knew he was only avoiding her eyes.

Her heartache was mixed with anger. It's your own fault, Simon Kent, she thought as she lifted her head very high. We were having such a wonderful time, and you ended it, just like that, without a word. I don't know if I'll ever forgive you.

At least he hadn't ruined Salem for her. She loved the campus, with its rolling green lawns, its huge old trees now beginning to bud, its old but sturdy brick and stone buildings, some covered with vines. She had felt at home here from the very first. And she had made so many other friends besides Simon.

"I'm sorry you're not going to the dance," Tobie told Quinn quietly as they walked back to the dorm that night. "I guess everyone still thinks you and Simon are an item. You could have asked someone, Quinn."

Quinn shook her head. "Not interested. And I don't want to talk about it. It's been a long day and I'm really tired." She forced a grin. "I don't think you have to worry about me waking you up tonight. I should sleep like the dead."

"I'm not worried. You've only walked in your sleep twice. Don't make it sound like you do it all the time."

"But I might," Quinn replied lightly, to hide the fear that had begun haunting her again, just as it had when she was in high school.

She couldn't believe it had started all over again.

Saturday was as busy as Friday, with a carnival out on the Commons. The events had been planned by Jessica Vogt and Ian Banion. They both lived at Nightingale Hall, an off-campus dorm a short distance from the university. A gloomy old brick house set high up on a hill, the place had been nicknamed "Nightmare Hall" following the tragic death of a girl who lived there.

Quinn liked both Jess and Ian. Jess was thin and pretty, with very short dark hair, and very nice. Ian was tall and good-looking, with shoulder-length hair the color of charcoal. They were a great couple.

All of it was fun. The hard part came later for Quinn, watching Tobie dress for the dance. And when a friend of theirs, Ivy Green, and her roommate, Suze Blythe, arrived from their room down the hall to "check out Tobie's dress," Quinn had to bite down hard on her lower lip to keep from crying out, "It's not fair! My first Spring Fling at Salem and I'm not even going to the big dance."

It's my own fault, she scolded silently. I was dumb enough to keep hoping until the last minute that Simon would recover from whatever was bugging him, and ask me. And he didn't. So here I am.

Ivy, her silky black hair swept sleekly away from her fair, oval face, said as she entered, "I can't believe you didn't invite someone to this dance, Quinn. I wouldn't have missed it for anything." Her tone of voice made it clear that fish would fly before Ivy Green sat alone in her room on a Saturday night.

Suze, who was short, with a great deal of blonde, curly hair, nodded. "Really, Quinn, you're not going to pine over Simon forever, are you?"

Quinn flushed. "I've got a handle on it," she said coolly. Right. Like anyone in the room believed that for a second.

"Simon Kent is a jerk," Ivy added emphatically.

"You could take *my* place at the dance," Tobie said softly. "I think I feel a headache coming on."

"Tobie!" Quinn sent her a stern glance. "Danny Collier's a nice guy. You'll have a great time."

"I know, but . . . I just don't feel like dancing." The look in Tobie's green eyes was one Quinn had seen before and couldn't identify. Sadness? Fear? Simple homesickness?

"You will when you get there," Ivy promised. "Now, let's get this show on the road. See you later, Quinn. If you wait up, we'll tell you all about it when we get home."

"Oh, I won't be up," Quinn said, flopping down on her bed. "I'll hit the books for a while, then it's an early bedtime for me. Have fun, you three."

She hated the look of pity in their eyes as they left the room.

She had only half-finished her paper when, although the night was warm, she was forced to get up and close the window to shut out the sounds of music coming from the dance.

She drew a stick figure, labeled it *Simon Kent*, stabbed it several dozen times with her pencil point and then, feeling better, threw the drawing away and finished her paper. Then she wrote briefly in her journal and went to bed, careful to remember her breathing exercises.

And she slept.

Chapter 2

It was warm in the ballroom of the Student Center. So many people gathered together in one space raised the temperature in spite of the big doors open on both sides. The floral decorations on the round tables were beginning to wilt like discarded lettuce leaves, and only a few black ties hadn't been stuffed into back pockets of black trousers, only a few white shirt collars remained firmly fastened.

The music of the last dance was slow. Couples filled the dance floor, entwined, heads lying on shoulders.

Had they been asked, most would have agreed that the evening had been great, fun, a blast, super, even . . . yes, even perfect.

But then it began.

It began slowly, entering the room in a mere whiff of . . . something different . . . something that didn't belong, that didn't fit.

A few noses wrinkled delicately and tried to dismiss it, reluctant to spoil the "perfect" evening by something that didn't fit.

But it wouldn't be dismissed.

It gathered strength, burgeoning quickly from a mere whiff to a definite presence that couldn't be ignored.

It began at a side wall, seeping out of a heat duct placed high above the floor. The people beneath the duct came to a sudden halt, as if stopped by a traffic cop. Coughing and choking broke out and eyes began to stream with tears as the foul odor enveloped them, wrapping them in its pungent fumes.

Leaving its mark on that group, it slithered further on into the room, dropping down to seize this couple, that couple, this group, that group, in its revolting grasp.

Shouts of "Oh, God, what *is* that?" sounded as feet stopped moving, eyes teared up, chests began to heave, hands flew to nostrils in an effort to escape the putrid smell.

Girls in brightly colored dresses stumbled backwards and guys in tuxedoes staggered helplessly as eyes were blinded by free-flowing tears from the sickening fumes. Bodies, spinning around in a frantic search for a way out, slammed into other bodies. Some fell to the worn wooden floor and were stepped on by other unseeing victims. Cries of pain echoed out into the huge room.

Members of the band, clutching their instruments, jumped down from the bandstand at the front of the room and raced for the open doors.

As the repugnant odor snaked its way into every corner of the room, the panic escalated into mayhem. Feet began running, pounding across the floorboards with urgency. Pushing and shoving were rampant. The smaller and weaker fell. Some were helped upright by others, some were not.

Jess and Ian stood in one corner and watched helplessly as the dance became a frenzied race for fresh, untainted air.

"It's like the running of the bulls," Jess said in disbelief, her own eyes beginning to tear as the foul odor reached their quiet little corner. "In Spain. When the bulls chase people down the street . . ."

Then they, too, were wrapped in the stinging, burning fumes, and were seized by the same need to escape them.

Halfway across the room, she fell, her arms instinctively reaching out to break her fall. As she landed, a heavy, racing foot came down hard on her left wrist. There was a sharp, snapping sound, like a twig being broken in half, and Jess screamed in pain. Ian bent to scoop her up off the floor and, scarcely breaking his stride, aimed for the door.

In the doorway jam, people were toppling like dominoes. Frightened voices cried out for help.

"Four at a time!" a voice shouted then, and a huge guy with blond hair appeared in the doorway, barring it, thick arms outstretched on each side of him. Danny Collier shouted commandingly, "You go out of here four at a time or you don't go at all!"

The stern command broke the panic. Realizing that people were being hurt, the crowd obeyed.

Although it seemed to take forever, the ballroom cleared.

They all gathered outside, wiping their eyes with tissues or hands, staring back at the student center in horrified disbelief.

Chapter 3

"What *was* it?" Tobie whispered to Danny when her eyes had stopped streaming. "What was that horrible smell?"

"Didn't you recognize it?" Ian asked, overhearing her. "From high school chem class? Sulfuric acid. Smells like rotten eggs, remember?" Having said that, he left to help a thoroughly shaken Jess to the infirmary. Other people with bumps and bruises or bloodied noses followed.

Ivy, wiping her face with a tissue, joined Tobie and Danny. Tim was right behind her, his tuxedo trousers torn at the pockets. "Our clothes are positively ruined!" Ivy cried with disgust. "Ruined! I paid two hundred dollars for this dress. Now I'm going to have to burn it. It smells like something in a landfill."

Tobie knew she was right. In spite of the

cool, fresh air, the vile stench still clung to their skin, their hair, their clothes. "Where could it have come from?"

Danny shrugged. "Who knows? But if Ian's right about it being sulfuric acid, I think someone should call the police."

"The police?" Suze and her date, a tall, thin boy named Leon, arrived, wiping their eyes. "You think we should call the police?"

"Well, it couldn't have been an accident," Danny said. "There's no chem lab in the Student Center. So my guess is, some nasty little amateur chemist rigged up a stink bomb and deliberately set it off."

Tobie and Ivy stared at him with reddened eyes. "What are you talking about?" Tobie said, a strained expression on her face. "You think someone ruined the dance on purpose?"

Danny's mouth was grim. "Can't be anything else. I'm calling the police."

By the time the police had taken everyone's dorm and room number and stopped asking questions, the desperate need for a hot, leisurely shower drew them all back to their rooms.

A small fortune in formal wear made its way to the incinerators that night.

When Quinn awoke the following morning,

Tobie was already awake, sitting upright on her bed, arms wrapped around her chest.

The first thing Quinn noticed was how red and swollen her roommate's eyes were.

Oh, no. Tobie hadn't had a good time? She hadn't really wanted to go. Had almost turned down Danny's invitation. It was Quinn who had urged her to accept, saying that Tobie didn't get out enough. Which was true.

But now she'd had a lousy time. So would she be mad at the person who had pushed her into going?

She didn't look mad. She looked . . . upset.

"What's wrong?" Quinn asked. "I thought you'd be sleeping late this morning."

Her eyes focused on the floor. Tobie didn't answer.

"What's wrong, Tobie? Didn't you have a good time?"

"It was okay," Tobie said then, lifting her head. "Until the last dance." And she told Quinn about the filthy, disgusting smell.

"I don't get it," Quinn said when Tobie had finished. "A smell? What kind of smell? Where did it come from?"

"It was that rotten egg smell. Sulfuric acid. Remember chem class in high school? You must have used it. We all did. Only this was horrible, so there must have been a lot of it. It was in our clothes, in our hair, on our skin. I showered for an hour when we got back." Tobie sighed heavily. "And we all had to burn our clothes."

Quinn was stunned. "Rotten eggs?" She had imagined them all having a wonderful time. She'd felt bad, even angry, that she wasn't a part of it. "Where did it come from?"

"No one knows yet. People think it was a stink bomb. The police are going to look into it."

The police? The police had been called to Salem's Spring Fling dance?

"Listen," Tobie said wearily, standing up, "I can still smell that awful stuff, even though I never brought my dress into this room and I showered before I came back. I guess I'll just have to keep showering and shampooing until I can't smell it anymore." She picked up a robe lying on the foot of her bed. "You should be glad you weren't there, Quinn. It really was horrible."

Looking frail and wan to Quinn, Tobie headed down the hall to the bathroom.

Quinn stayed in bed, trying to digest what she'd been told.

A smell had ruined the dance? A foul stench

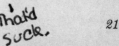

21

that had caused people to panic and run and people had gotten hurt? "Like a stampede," Tobie had said, "in some old western."

Crazy. Totally crazy. *Totally, Totally crazy*

Where would a smell like that have come from?

Quinn got up and went to the window. The whole campus would be buzzing about the dance's disaster. It was Sunday. No classes. A beautiful, sunny, spring day. People would be gossiping, all right, but they'd also be sunning and jogging, and gathering on the Commons, a grassy green area in the middle of campus.

She was suddenly anxious to get outside and find out if anyone knew anything more about the disaster that had taken place at the dance.

Turning, she hurried to the closet and pulled the door open.

Grouch. And recoiled in revulsion at the odor that slapped her in the face. It was overpowering. There was no mistaking what it was. The smell of rotten eggs.

Her eyes began to water.

But . . . Tobie had said she'd burned her dress. That she'd never brought it back into this room. And she had showered and shampooed for an hour before she came back here.

Maybe she'd hung her jacket from last night in the closet. Throwing away a jacket as well as a new dress might have been too much for her. Or maybe her purse was in there, or the shoes she'd worn.

Whatever it was, it had to be taken out of the closet, or everything in there would have to be burned.

Gathering her courage and placing a hand over her nose, Quinn moved on into the closet. And realized very quickly that the odor was coming from *her* side of the closet.

It had been late when Tobie came in, and dark. She must have mistakenly hung her jacket on Quinn's side.

Then a small kernel of uneasiness began to stir within Quinn. Because the fact was, Tobie Thomason never hung *anything* in the closet when she came home from anywhere. She never hung up anything, period. She was a dropper. How likely was it that she'd suddenly reformed last night of all nights?

By checking each article, Quinn was able to single out one garment as being the sole source of the odor.

It was a bright red jacket.

But it wasn't Tobie's. It was *hers*.

A favorite jacket, lightweight enough for warm fall days, but warm enough for cooler nights. She wore it often.

She hadn't *gone* to that dance. So how could

a jacket of hers possibly carry the disgusting odor of rotten eggs? It's a mystery!

Impossible.

But this jacket had to have been at that dance, Quinn thought, yanking it off its hanger, holding it as far away from her as possible. Where else would it have been contaminated with that smell?

Still holding the jacket at arm's length, she hurried to the door. Out in the quiet hall, she headed straight for the incinerator chute.

The jacket couldn't have gone to the dance without her. She would have heard if someone had come into her room and taken it, wouldn't she? Tobie had worn a pale pink dress, so she would never have borrowed a red jacket to wear. Her jacket, Quinn remembered, had been black.

Quinn opened the incinerator door and threw the red jacket down the chute. The stench wafted back up into her face, and her eyes teared anew.

She felt sick, but she wasn't sure it was simply from the smell. Her favorite red jacket had left her room last night. And because she was Quinn Hadley, who had a sleeping disorder, she couldn't be absolutely, positively certain that she hadn't been *inside* that jacket when it left her room. And because she was Quinn Hadley-who-had-a-sleeping-disorder, she couldn't be absolutely positive that she hadn't *gone* to that dance.

What was worse was, if she *had* gone, she had no idea what she'd done when she got there.

Oh no!

Chapter 4

When Tobie came back from the bathroom, Quinn was standing at the window again, looking down on the Commons. It was beginning to fill up with people. There were tennis matches scheduled for that afternoon between the Salem tennis teams and members of a group of visiting alumni. A picnic was to be held on the Commons, and for those who liked neither tennis nor picnics, boat rides were available on the Salem River, behind the University.

"It doesn't look any different down there," Quinn commented when she heard the bathroom door open. "You'd never guess the dance was ruined last night."

"Well, you'd know it in *here*," Tobie complained. "I can still smell that stuff. I don't get it. I have scrubbed and scrubbed and shampooed every inch of my scalp. And I burned my dress. But it still stinks in this room."

Quinn, her back still to Tobie, flushed guiltily. The red jacket. Although it was gone now, it had been in the closet, probably for hours. No wonder the smell lingered.

"It's warm enough to open the windows," she said as she turned around. Avoiding Tobie's eyes, she went directly to the closet and began yanking clothes off hangers. "Everything in this closet smells. If we open the windows wide and scatter our clothes around the room, maybe the fresh air will help."

"Well," Tobie grumbled, "I don't understand why our closet smells. I didn't hang anything in there last night." But when she got close enough to the hanging clothing, she gasped. "Whew! You're right." She sighed. "I guess it's just the kind of smell that gets into everything."

When they had scattered their clothing around the room, Tobie shrugged. "At least now it's not just my side of the room that looks bad. If anyone walked in here now, they'd think we were *both* slobs."

Quinn waited nervously for Tobie to ask why the closet stank.

But Tobie, anxious to leave the room and get outside, continued to dress without asking any more questions.

She thinks it's *her*, Quinn realized. Tobie's

convinced that because I wasn't at the dance, *she's* the one who brought the odor home with her.

I should tell her, Quinn thought.

But she didn't. Naughty girl!

Because before she could explain it to Tobie, she had to be able to explain it to *herself*. And she couldn't. Not yet. She had no idea how the red jacket had picked up the smell of rotten eggs from a dance she hadn't attended.

She *hadn't*, had she?

Quinn tied the laces on her sneakers and thrust her straight, dark hair up into a bouncy ponytail. She never remembered her sleep-walking episodes. Someone always had to tell her about them. First, her parents and her younger sister, Sophie, and now, Tobie. "You were sleepwalking last night, Quinn." She always had the same reaction: disbelief, and then dismay that she'd done something she couldn't remember.

She did remember two episodes, because they'd ended badly. The first happened when she was fourteen and Sophie was twelve. They'd had a fight earlier in the day and hadn't made it up. They'd gone to bed angry. Some-time in the middle of the night, Quinn had been jerked rudely awake by her parents pulling her away from Sophie's bed where, they told her in shocked voices, she'd been pummeling her younger sister, using her fists.

The incident had terrified Quinn. She had never deliberately hurt anyone in her life, and she hated violence of any kind. She didn't want to believe it was true. But the looks on her parents' faces and the fear in Sophie's eyes didn't lie.

The second incident had happened two years later, at a summer camp where Quinn was a counselor. She had lost a tennis match to a girl she couldn't stand, an arrogant, unpleasant fellow counselor. The girl had been insufferable in her win, laughing at Quinn and taking as an added trophy the boy Quinn had had her eyes on since they'd arrived. Go girl!

A senior counselor had found her that time. According to him, Quinn had been crouched behind the girl's cabin in the dark at two in the morning. Using a rock as a hammer, she was deliberately, methodically, destroying the very expensive tennis racket that had been left outside.

Although Quinn, abruptly awakened, hadn't remembered why she was at the cabin or what she'd been doing, she had been sent home. That was when her mother had taken her to the psychiatrist. He had explained to Quinn then exactly what had happened, and suggested that she was simply acting out in her sleep anger that she was too timid to express openly when she was awake.

That was probably true. The Hadley household frowned on any kind of openly expressed disagreement. "Least said, soonest mended" was her family's credo. She had learned it early.

Last night, hadn't she been angry that Simon hadn't asked her to the Spring Fling dance? Hadn't she been angry that she'd missed one of the biggest formal dances at Salem?

How angry?

Quinn fastened tiny pale pink rose earrings in her lobes. Angry enough to leave her room in the middle of the night, wearing the red jacket? Angry enough to make her way across campus to the student center and . . .

And do *what*?

Rotten eggs . . . sulfuric acid . . .

She had been very good in chem in high school. She had especially liked the experiments. Combining one chemical with another and watching the resulting reaction had been fun. She hadn't found the symbols or the equations confusing like a lot of kids had.

Yes, she had been very good in chemistry.

"We'll have to do a load of laundry when we come back," Tobie said as they left the clothes-cluttered room. "I used the last towel. Seems like we just washed towels, but there aren't any more clean ones in the closet. I think we're missing a couple. You haven't left any in someone else's room, have you?"

"No." But . . . she had been wondering why, if she actually *had* gone to the dance in her sleep, her hair and her skin didn't smell, as Tobie said hers had. The missing towels could explain that. Maybe she'd come home and showered and shampooed before going back to bed. And then maybe she had burned the towels in the same incinerator that had swallowed up the red jacket.

This is crazy, Quinn scolded herself as they stepped into the elevator. It smelled faintly of rotten eggs. What am I *doing*? I'm making myself nuts here, writing a whole scenario that probably never even happened. I'd remember walking across campus to that dance. I *would*.

But she hadn't remembered punching Sophie.

Or wrecking the tennis racket.

Although there seemed to be food everywhere on campus, tables of it on the Commons, at the tennis matches, more tables down by the boat dock along the river, Quinn had no appetite. She ate nothing.

Simon and Danny Collier won the canoe race.

Quinn stood off to one side, watching as Jessica Vogt and Ian Banion handed Simon his small brass trophy. Jess's left wrist was in a white cast to her elbow.

Quinn found that frightening. People had *really* been hurt at that dance. Small wonder everyone was talking about it. And she had felt the gloom of it all day. Although the weather was warm and sunny, people seemed to be trying too hard to enjoy it. Smiles looked forced, and what laughter there was sounded artificial.

She wondered if Simon had gone to the dance. She hadn't worked up the nerve yet to ask anyone. It would have seemed petty and self-centered to ask such a question following Tobie's incredible story. It wasn't important. What difference did it make if Simon had gone to the dance? He hadn't gone with *her* and wasn't that all she needed to know?

Still, if he *had* gone, she would be interested in his take on what had happened. Simon was incredibly smart, very aware. That's what had drawn her to him in the first place. He had been in town at Vinnie's one night, eating pizza with a group of friends. She'd passed by his booth just as he was giving his opinion of athletes using steroids and she'd been impressed by what he said. It wasn't just that he was against it, as she was. It was the clear, objective, intelligent way he presented his arguments. He'd even managed to get a laugh or two.

She liked the way he looked, too. He was too thin, maybe because he was so tall, and his posture was terrible. But he had clear gray eyes, sun-streaked sandy hair needing a trim, and a strong chin. When he got the laughs he wanted, she had watched from across the room as his mouth curved into a satisfied grin.

She had introduced herself to him an hour later, when they'd both finished eating and he was standing at the jukebox alone.

It was stupid to keep avoiding him now. Or was it the other way around? Was *he* avoiding *her*?

Whatever. So they weren't going out anymore. So she had no idea why. Did that mean they couldn't even be friends? Simon was smart and funny and he'd been sympathetic about the sleepwalking when she'd told him. It had seemed wrong to keep something that important in her life from Simon.

She missed him.

Taking a deep breath, she strode over to the edge of the dock and, lifting her chin, said heartily, "Congratulations, Simon. Great race!" Ivy, standing nearby, smiled approval. Her dark eyes signaled, "It's about time you took the initiative."

Simon looked surprised. His face and arms were sunburned, so she couldn't tell if he was flushing. But at least he didn't run away. "Thanks. Danny's dynamite with a paddle."

"Don't be so modest. You won the race together. That *is* a trophy you're holding, right?"

Simon laughed. "Yeah, I guess it is."

Ivy led Tim, Danny, Tobie, and Suze away, leaving Simon and Quinn alone together.

"Not very subtle, are they?" Quinn remarked. "So, did you go to the dance last night?" That *was* why she'd come over here to talk to him, wasn't it?

"No!" He frowned at her. "Of course not."

Of course not? What did *that* mean? Of course not as in, Not without *you*, I didn't?

You *wish*, she told herself.

"Did you?" he asked.

The crowd began to disperse. They were standing alone on the dock, the sun beginning to slip toward the horizon. The day was almost over.

"No." At least, she added mentally, I don't *think* I did. "I thought if you were there, maybe you could tell me what happened. I mean, *how* you think it happened, and maybe why. It sounded horrible."

Simon shook his head. "Beats me. I heard the police found a stink bomb with a timing device. Which means the person who set it off could have been anywhere when it happened — even out there dancing like everyone else."

They began walking along the river path. "So it wasn't accidental," Quinn commented.

"Accidental? There's no chem lab in the Student Center. How could it have been accidental?"

Well, he didn't need to bite her head off. What was rattling his cage, anyway?

"Who would do something so nasty?" she wondered aloud.

Simon said he had no idea who might have done it. Nor did he have any idea *why* someone would do something so nasty.

When he'd said quickly, "See you later," and hurried off, Quinn stood beside the river, watching him go. She felt very lonely suddenly, and very uneasy.

Because *she* knew a reason why someone might do something so nasty.

Someone might do something so nasty because they were very, very angry about not attending the dance.

They might not want to, and they might not mean to, but maybe they hadn't known exactly what they were doing. Maybe they hadn't had any control over it, like someone who was compulsive, psychotic, someone who couldn't help him or herself. Or someone who did things in her sleep that she couldn't remember later.

Chapter 5

For the next three nights, Quinn took the precaution of wearing clean white socks to bed. She would check each morning to see if they were dirty. If they were, that would be a clear sign that she'd been wandering around the dorm during the night.

All three mornings, the socks were as clean as when she'd slipped them on.

Her relief was overwhelming.

On campus, the talk centered around Spring Fling, specifically the dance. The police had indeed found a giant stink bomb with a timing device, but no one seemed to have any idea who the guilty party might be. The investigation was ongoing.

"Suze thinks it was a bad joke, but I don't," Tobie told Quinn on Wednesday. They were at the library, seated in a quiet corner by a window. "I think someone deliberately ruined the dance because they were mad that they didn't get to go."

This struck so close to Quinn's deepest fear that she snapped, "That's ridiculous. Anyone who wanted to go to that dance could have gone." She gave her roommate a sharp glance, wondering if Tobie had been hinting at something.

How could she have been? She didn't know about the red jacket.

Later, they wandered over to the baseball diamond to watch practice. They weren't the only ones who saw the bleachers as a great place to relax and catch some sun. Ivy and Suze were there, surrounded by several boys, as always. And Quinn spotted Simon, sitting at the very top of the stands.

He wasn't alone. There was a girl with him, a tall, very pretty blonde in a cheerleader's uniform. Her name, Quinn thought, was Delle.

Pain stabbed her at the sight of Simon with another girl. She quickly turned her attention to Tobie. "So," she said casually as she opened a math notebook, "how are things with you and Danny?"

Tobie shrugged, her eyes aimed straight ahead of her, toward the field below. "He's okay. Danny's great, but I'm not interested. Guys are a waste of time."

It was the most cynical thing Quinn had ever heard her say. She didn't know how to respond. "Tobie? What's wrong?"

Tobie ran a hand through her short red hair and shook her head. "Nothing," she said, glancing sideways at Quinn. "Sorry." Then she looked back at the field again.

But not before Quinn saw the shiny glint of tears in Tobie's green eyes.

"Ivy and Suze have the right idea," Tobie went on. "Ivy doesn't just date Tim Lobo, even though he's nuts about her. She's not about to tie herself down to one guy. And Suze plays the field, too. Safer that way." She shrugged her thin shoulders. "But Danny's nice, and fun. Like I said, he's okay."

Quinn glanced down at the field. Danny looked up just then, saw them, and waved.

"He likes you, Tobie. It's obvious."

Tobie smiled and returned the wave. "I was in love once," she said quietly. "I thought it was forever. You know how you are in high school. You think everything's forever. Only it isn't."

She was dumped, Quinn thought. And it hurt a lot. That's why she's moody, that's why she's so quiet, why she hardly ever dates. I wonder what she was like before it happened?

Ivy and Suze, minus their admirers, joined

them then, their cheeks pink from the sun. "Men are pigs," Ivy announced flatly, directing a wicked gaze up the bleachers at Simon. "Is that or is it not Simon Kent up there with Delle Arlen?"

Before a red-faced Quinn could respond, Tobie leaned forward and asked Ivy about an assignment they shared. The conversation became general, and Quinn was grateful.

Maybe Ivy, Suze, and Tobie were right. Simon Kent could go take a flying leap. Quinn Hadley had more important things on her mind.

Forcing a brilliant smile, she joined the conversation.

After practice, they walked down the road to the long, silver diner called Burgers Etc. Danny, his blond hair still damp from a shower, joined them, and then, his dark hair blowing in the breeze, Tim Lobo hurried over to invite himself along.

The diner was midway between the university and the town. Being so close to campus, Burgers was the most popular restaurant in the area, with Vinnie's Pizzeria running a close second.

It seemed to Quinn as she sat in their booth waiting for her food, that the entire restaurant was filled with couples. There was only one other big group like theirs. The other blue booths were filled with couples hanging all over each other.

Quinn knew one of the couples. Carlie Winters and Donner Timms, both sophomores. They'd been going together since their freshman year and Quinn hardly ever saw one without the other.

Watching Quinn watching, Tobie said suddenly, "It won't last. Any of it. It's like the dance the other night . . . it started off just great. But then," her mouth turned downward, "just like that, it was ruined. Ruined!"

An awkward silence followed her remark.

"I'm sorry," she whispered, and jumped up and ran out of the diner.

Danny stared at Tobie's retreating back. "What's with her?" he asked in a bewildered voice. "I can't figure her out."

"You don't know what happened to her?" Tim said.

Quinn sat up straighter. Tim knew something about Tobie? "I don't," she said. "What happened to Tobie?"

"Her boyfriend died. Last year. Right after Christmas."

Quinn gasped. Ivy's eyes widened, Suze whispered, "Oh, no," and Danny stared.

"Died?" Ivy asked. "How? Car wreck?"

Tim shook his head. "I don't know. I don't think it was a car wreck. All I know is, they were planning on going to college together, maybe even getting married first, but he didn't make it. And Tobie took it really hard, that's what I heard."

"Where?" Quinn said. "Where did you hear it?" She couldn't believe Tim Lobo knew something about Tobie that Tobie hadn't even told her own roommate.

"Some guy from Tobie's hometown. Riverdale. He went to school with Tobie and her boyfriend. But if you're looking for details," Tim added, "you won't get them from him. He left. He decided to go into his father's business. He's gone."

Quinn sat frozen in shock. Tobie hadn't been dumped. That wasn't why she seemed so depressed, and so cynical. The guy she'd loved had *died*.

Quinn couldn't take it all in. She tried to imagine losing someone you loved. What would that do to you?

Tobie had said disparagingly of herself, "I'm no barrel of laughs." How *could* she be, after what she'd been through?

Why hadn't she said anything?

I would have understood, Quinn thought. I would have. And been sympathetic.

But . . . maybe Tobie didn't want sympathy. Maybe she'd come to Salem to pick up the pieces of her life, make a new start, and didn't want people knowing the whole awful story.

If Tobie didn't want to talk about it, no one should force her to.

But, Quinn thought, now that I know, it's going to be hard not to bring it up. And I thought it was a soured romance that hurt Tobie, she thought sadly. It wasn't. It was *death*.

Her appetite gone, and anxious to see if Tobie was okay, Quinn excused herself and hurried back to the dorm.

Tobie wasn't there.

She called while Quinn was finishing up her homework, saying that she was at Nightingale Hall with a friend, Cath Devon. She sounded perfectly normal. She said she was working on a project with Cath and wouldn't be home until late. Might even stay the night.

Quinn said nothing about what she'd learned from Tim.

Tobie couldn't be too depressed, Quinn told herself, or she wouldn't be considering spending the night at *Nightmare* Hall. Such a gloomy old house! Rumor had it that some very strange things had gone on in that place.

Chapter 6

The couple sat on a bench on a lower terrace of the Tower, a tall, narrow structure of buff-colored bricks sitting in the center of Salem's campus. The terraces, several of them high enough to provide an impressive view, were favorite hangout spots when the weather was nice. The lower level where the couple sat was partially sheltered from above by an identical balcony jutting out from the fourth floor. Lights from offices in the building eased the darkness with a soft, warm glow.

The air was warm, the breeze gentle as, heads together, the two talked and laughed, sipping soda as they talked from brightly labeled paper cups.

When the cups were empty they got up in silent agreement, cups in hand, and walked to the barrel-shaped trash container in one un-sheltered corner of the terrace.

The girl pushed the swinging lid inward. Her companion tossed his cup into the yawning mouth of the trash container.

She was about to toss hers in when a faint sound from above brought her head up, tilted backward, and her eyes flew open as she saw a thick stream of liquid cascading down upon them.

She had only enough time to cry out, "What . . . ?" before the thick, warm goo slopped down over their hair, their faces, coating the eyes, the nose, the mouth, the skin, sliding on down across the throat, the shoulders, the arms, the hands. The sludge coated their lashes. They blinked rapidly, unable to see. They spat fiercely, trying to dislodge the ooze from mouths that had been open in surprise, but the liquid clung stubbornly to teeth and tongue.

"Paint," the girl managed in a thick, astonished voice, "paint!"

They were covered from head to toe with an overcoat of thick, odorous paint.

Hands gloved in what they could see now was a vibrant red color, they batted helplessly at their faces, their hair, their clothes, rubbing and swatting in vain at the warm, sticky goo.

As they stood there, desperately trying to free themselves, a sound from above brought their sticky, scarlet heads up a second time, their paint-reddened eyes wide with dread.

But all they heard was a slow, mechanical laugh drifting out into the night air.

Then silence.

Chapter 7

Ivy awoke Quinn and Tobie the following morning with an insistent rapping on their door. "Wake up, you two!" she cried, "and let me in. I bring news. You've *gotta* hear this!"

"*What?*" Quinn snapped when she'd opened the door. She had a headache and the feeling that she hadn't slept very well. She had had a terrible dream, in which she had walked into her room late at night and found Simon lying unconscious on the floor. The feeling that she was somehow responsible had overwhelmed her, and she'd awakened shaking. Her mouth tasted like sandpaper, her eyes were gritty, and here was Ivy, fully dressed, at what had to be the crack of dawn. Suze was standing behind her in a bathrobe, looking bewildered.

"Don't tell me, let me guess," Quinn said, retreating back to her bed and slumping down on it as Tobie roused sleepily. "You've just been asked out by Kevin Costner. News at eleven."

"It's not funny," Ivy said, glowering at Quinn. She plopped down on the floor, legs stretched out in front of her, back against Tobie's bed. Suze collapsed beside Tobie. "Carlie Winters and Donner Timms were drenched with red paint last night on the first-floor terrace of the Tower."

Quinn gasped. Tobie sat up very straight. "What?" they cried in one voice.

Ivy nodded. "They're both at the infirmary even as I speak. It was slopped down on them from one of the higher terraces. They had paint in their hair, their eyes, their mouths . . ." Ivy shuddered. "It sounds horrible. I saw Meg Pekoe out in the hall and she said that stuff can make you sick. I mean, after all, you're not supposed to *bathe* in it!"

Quinn found her voice. "Paint? Red paint? Why would someone be painting the tower *red*?"

"No one's painting the tower, Quinn," Ivy said flatly. "Someone went up there with a bucket of paint and dumped it on Carlie and Donner. On *purpose*!"

Quinn and Tobie exchanged shocked glances. Someone had taken a bucket of paint up into

48

the tower and deliberately doused Carlie and Donner with it?

"Why?" Tobie said aloud. "Why would someone do that?"

Ivy shrugged. "Who knows? We still haven't figured out why someone would set off a stink bomb at the Spring Fling dance, have we? Maybe Carlie or Donner has some idea about who might have paint-bombed them. If they do, we won't find out about it today. Meg told me Carlie's eyes are a mess from all that paint. She won't be going to any of her classes."

Quinn sat quietly, lost in dismal thought. She was remembering Carlie and Donner at Vinnie's. They had looked so happy.

Apparently someone hadn't liked that.

Could it have been the same someone who'd ruined the Spring Fling dance for other happy couples?

When Quinn glanced over at Tobie again, she was surprised to see her roommate's eyes filling with tears.

"It's awful," Tobie whispered, "it's just awful." Then she slid off the bed and headed out to the bathroom.

Suze nodded. "She's right. It *is* awful."

Ivy stood up. "It seems like whenever we talk about couples now, Tobie goes a little ballistic. I guess it makes her think about that guy she dated in high school. I mean, Tim did say they were nuts about each other, right? She probably still misses him."

Quinn nodded silently. "I guess."

When Ivy and Suze had gone back to their room, Quinn lay on her bed staring up at the ceiling. Carlie and Donner hadn't really been hurt. Not seriously. But it must have been so horrible, being showered with sticky, oily red paint. She had painted her bedroom peach one summer, and her parents had warned her not to get any paint in her eyes and to keep the room well-ventilated so she didn't breathe in the fumes, and to shower thoroughly when she was done. Ivy was right. It certainly wasn't healthy to be *bathed* in paint, as Carlie and Donner had been.

Maybe they hadn't been seriously hurt. But whoever had dumped that paint on them certainly hadn't intended to do them any *good*, either.

Why would someone *do* something so nasty?

Sighing, Quinn got up and went to the closet. A cloudy day outside, but it was probably still warm. The white poet's blouse, maybe the short denim skirt.

Had Carlie's eyes been permanently affected by the paint? How many classes would she have to miss? Missing just one or two lectures at college could screw up your grade point average.

Where was the white blouse? It had been hanging right there, between the green striped rugby shirt and her white terrycloth robe.

The denim skirt wasn't on her skirt hanger, either.

Had she worn them, tossed them in the laundry, and forgotten?

No. She distinctly remembered seeing them hanging in the closet yesterday.

Carlie and Donner had looked so happy at Vinnie's. It had made Quinn miss Simon even more than she usually did. And now, today, they were at the infirmary, probably still trying to get the last few traces of red paint off their skin.

The denim skirt couldn't have slipped free of the tight metal clamps on the skirt hanger, but the blouse might have slipped from its blue plastic hanger and fallen to the floor of the closet. Quinn crouched, searching the floor of the closet with her eyes.

There . . . at the back of the closet, a ball of something white. Puffy sleeves . . . her white blouse. And beside it, also crumpled, the denim skirt. How on earth had that skirt slipped free of those metal clamps?

Quinn knelt, and leaning forward, reached

into the shadowy depths of the closet, pulling the two articles of clothing toward her. When she had both of them in hand, she backed out of the closet and stood up, tossing the skirt over her shoulder as she held up the white blouse to check for wrinkle damage.

And recoiled in horror as she unfolded the garment.

Red, bright, vibrant splotches of red, splashed all up and down the front of the blouse, as if someone had used it as a canvas for an abstract painting.

Gasping in horror, Quinn threw it to the floor and stood staring down at it as if she'd never seen it before and didn't know how it had arrived in her hands.

Tentatively, her mouth tense, Quinn pulled the skirt off her shoulder and held that, too, out in front of her.

More red, a river of it running from waist to hem.

The doorknob turned.

Breathing in short gasps, Quinn snatched the blouse up from the floor, balled both garments into tiny bundles and thrust them under her bed.

Tobie came into the room, a towel wrapped turban-style around her red hair. "You okay?" she asked as Quinn, her legs weak, sank down upon her bed. "Still upset about Carlie and Donner? I don't blame you. It's horrible, just plain horrible."

"Tobie," Quinn said when she trusted herself to speak, "what time did you get in last night?"

"About midnight. Why?"

"I just wondered. I didn't hear you come in."

"Well, of course not, Quinn. You never hear anything once you've gone to sleep. You were out like a light when I came in."

Quinn breathed easier. She'd been asleep when Tobie came in. Tobie had just said so. Safely asleep, in her bed . . . not wandering around campus dumping paint on innocent, happy people.

Not that she had seriously thought it could have been her. The doctor had said she was expressing anger when she did those things in her sleep. She wasn't angry at Carlie or Donner. Why *would* she be?

But . . . she *had* gone to sleep angry. She did remember that. Angry at . . . ? What was it that had made her angry?

Oh. She remembered now. The story about what had happened to Tobie. She'd been upset about that.

But that had nothing to do with Carlie or Donner.

Quinn got up and walked over to the dresser

mirror. As she picked up a hairbrush and began slowly brushing her straight brown hair, she could see Tobie moving from bed to closet and back again. The expression on her face was sad.

Was she thinking about Carlie and Donner? Or about something much, much worse . . . was Tobie thinking now about what had happened to her before she ever came to Salem?

"Could I borrow your blue denim skirt?" Tobie asked suddenly, turning toward Quinn. "If you're not going to wear it, I mean."

In the mirror, Quinn watched as her cheeks flamed scarlet. As red as the paint on the skirt Tobie was asking to borrow. "It's . . . it's in the laundry," she stammered.

"No, it isn't. I washed it last week with my stuff. I remember because I was really careful to take it out of the dryer at exactly the right time, so it wouldn't wrinkle. I know how you hate to iron stuff."

"Yeah, I know, but I was going to wear it yesterday, and then I spilled nail polish on it. Sorry. You can wear my navy skirt if you want. It's clean."

"Darn. Thanks anyway, but that skirt's too dressy. I want something I can wear with socks. I'll just wear jeans."

Socks.

Quinn glanced down at her feet. She'd forgotten about the clean white socks she'd been wearing to bed every night. If she'd left her bed last night, the bottoms wouldn't be snowy white anymore, would they? Wasn't that why she'd begun wearing them in the first place . . . thinking they'd tell the story? And now, when she was worried, she hadn't even bothered to check them out. She'd forgotten.

Her heart pounding loudly in her chest, she hurried back to the bed and sat down. She didn't want to look. She *did* want to look. She did, she didn't . . .

She lifted her foot and twisted her leg sideways.

The soles of her socks were still clean. Pure, snowy white.

Letting out a deep sigh of relief, Quinn let her foot drop.

She hadn't walked in her sleep last night. She hadn't left her bed, her room, hadn't left Devereaux and found a huge can of paint and carried it up to the tower and dumped it on people.

Of course she hadn't.

But . . . if she hadn't gone wandering last night . . . if she'd stayed in her bed from the moment she got into it until Ivy and Suze arrived this morning . . . if that was true, then . . .

Where had the red paint come from on her white blouse and blue denim skirt?

Deciding she couldn't stay in her room all day and go crazy wondering what was going on, Quinn dressed quickly in jeans and a gray university sweatshirt. She snaked one foot under the bed to drag her sneakers forward.

The left one emerged, lying on its side. The foot went back in and pulled out the right shoe.

It wasn't lying on its side. It was sitting upright, laces untied.

But it was no longer the all-white shoe she had discarded the night before.

Now, like the white blouse and the denim skirt, the white sneaker wore huge ragged splotches of bright red, as if it were bleeding.

Quinn stared down at the shoe, her mouth hanging loosely open, her blue eyes silvery with unshed tears. And she knew why her socks were still as clean as when she'd donned them the night before.

Because if she *had* gone somewhere in her sleep last night, she hadn't gone in her socks.

This time, she had put on her shoes.

Chapter 8

Quinn had no idea how she got through her classes that day. Everywhere she went on campus, people were talking about Carlie and Donner. There were a dozen different theories about why it had happened. Someone knew a girl who had a thing for Donner and was jealous of Carlie . . . maybe *she* had done it. There was this guy on the basketball team who had been following Carlie around . . . maybe *he* had done it. Someone knew a practical joker who was always looking for stunts to pull and probably thought dumping paint on people would be a hoot. Maybe *he* had done it.

It was all speculation. No one knew anything for certain. Security guards in Salem uniforms were everywhere, asking questions. But no one seemed to have any definite answers.

Quinn was haunted by the dreadful possibility that she might be the one person on campus who had the answer.

She met Ivy and Tobie for lunch, but none of them ate anything. Tobie's face was pale and pinched-looking, and Ivy looked tired, her usual energy not in evidence.

They were on the way out of the dining hall when Quinn spotted Simon coming toward them. She could tell by the look on his face that he'd already seen them. His mouth was as straight-edged as a ruler, his cheeks slightly flushed. He was carrying a package from the mall sports shop.

New sneakers probably, Quinn thought testily. The better to run away from Quinn Hadley.

He passed the trio with a mumbled "hey." But Quinn, red-faced, had taken only a few steps when he called out softly, "Quinn? See you a minute?"

"Go ahead," Ivy urged as Quinn hesitated. "Catch up with us later." Then she grabbed Tobie's elbow and pulled her away, leaving no room for Quinn to argue.

When she turned to face Simon, he was standing under a huge old oak tree, its new leaves just starting to emerge. "I just wanted to make sure you were okay. After what happened to Carlie and Donner, I thought you might be a little shaky."

"It was awful," she admitted. Then she remembered the abrupt way Simon had left her life and became angry all over again. "But I really don't see how my feelings concern you. I mean, you've made it very clear that you're not interested, right?"

Instantly, she wanted to kick herself. Hadn't she *promised* herself that she wouldn't ask him what had happened? And now here she was, making a big deal out of a simple question from him. Fool!

"*I'm* not interested?" Simon's thick, sandy eyebrows married in a frown. "I'm not the one who wrote the letter, am I?"

It was Quinn's turn to look puzzled. "Letter? What letter?"

Simon withdrew a brown wallet from the inside pocket of his light blue windbreaker. "The letter you wrote telling me you didn't want to see me or talk to me. I have it right here." Unfolding the wallet, he reached in and pulled free a sheet of bright pink paper folded into a small square.

Quinn didn't own bright pink stationery. But the paper in Simon's hand did look vaguely familiar. "That's not from me," she said.

"What are you talking about?" Simon asked.

"You signed it. See," unfolding the letter and pointing, "right there! *Quinn*. You're the only Quinn on campus as far as I know, and you're definitely the only Quinn who would be writing to me."

"Let me see that." Quinn stretched out a hand and Simon gave her the letter. She read the typewritten note quickly.

Simon,
I know we've had a lot of fun, but now it's time to move on. I don't want to be tied down to just one person and you shouldn't, either. As for staying friends, that never works. Let's just say we had a good time and leave it at that, okay? I see no point in any further contact between us. Have a good life.

Quinn

nice note

"I never wrote this!" she said quietly. "And you should have known I didn't. It doesn't sound anything like me, Simon." She quoted: " '*I see no point in any further contact between us*'? Simon, I would never say something like that. It sounds like I'm firing an employee, not ending a relationship. Besides," she added, lifting her head to look Simon squarely in the face,

"I *didn't* want to stop seeing you, so why would I write this in the first place?"

"You didn't write this?" Simon asked. "You didn't *write* this?"

"I didn't write it," Quinn repeated softly. "I wouldn't have. Why didn't you *ask* me?"

"Because," he tapped the pink paper with one finger, "you said *not* to."

"Well, you could have *fought* a little harder," Quinn said tartly. "Are you that easy to get rid of?"

"If I were," he responded just as tartly, "I wouldn't be standing here now, would I?"

Good point.

Relenting, Quinn dropped her books on the ground, smiled, reached up, and wrapped her arms around Simon's neck.

She couldn't see his face then, to see if he was returning the smile, but it was clear that he was returning the hug.

And a minute later, he punctuated the hug with a man-am-I-glad-you're-back kiss.

Which Quinn returned with a heartfelt how-could-you-be-so-dumb kiss.

A few minutes later, they were sitting on the low stone wall encircling the fountain on the Commons.

The only thing Simon knew about the letter was that it had been pushed underneath the door to his room. He'd found it when he came home one afternoon.

"I've seen that paper before," Quinn told him. "I just can't remember where. Why would someone do something so mean?" She glanced at Simon. "Who were you dating before I came along?"

"No one special. Although . . ." Simon grinned, "there is this tall blonde in chem class who smiles at me a lot."

Quinn rolled her eyes. "I'm serious. I want to know how this happened. It was a really mean thing to do, and I can't think of anyone who hates me that much."

"Maybe," Simon said thoughtfully, "it was the same person who set off that stink bomb and went after Carlie and Donner. Someone who hates to see any couples happy together."

As bizarre as the thought seemed to be, Simon had a point. But his mention of Carlie and Donner caused a small snake of uneasiness to slither up her spine as she remembered the paint-stained clothing hidden in her room.

Should she tell him? He knew about the sleepwalking. Maybe he could reassure her, convince her that she hadn't been anywhere near the tower when that paint rained down upon Carlie and Donner. But what if he didn't? What if he thought that maybe she *had* done it?

Poor Simon. He didn't know what he was getting into, dating a somnambulist. Fancy word for a real pain-in-the-neck condition. And maybe it was worse than just annoying, or frightening. Maybe it was dangerous.

She wasn't going to let it spoil her reunion with Simon. She'd worry about the hidden clothing and shoes later. Right now, for a change, she was going to relax and have fun.

She did just that. They walked over to the stadium to watch football practice and afterwards went to the mall with Tobie and Danny, where they ran into Ivy and Tim, and Suze and Leon. Any time one of the group started to bring up the subject of what had happened to Carlie and Donner, Quinn quickly and fiercely shushed them. She refused to think about it.

Later, they drove to a club in town called Johnny's Place where Salem students gathered because it was one of the few places that had dancing.

Her arms around Simon on the dimly lit dance floor, Quinn closed her mind to everything but the moment, until her feet began to hurt in the black flats. When she suggested a

63

little while later that they call it a night, only Suze argued. "It's way too early," she complained, pouting. But she was overruled. They'd all had a busy week.

Back in their room at Devereaux, Quinn watched as Tobie tossed a toothbrush into her tote bag. She had decided to spend the night at Nightingale Hall again, saying she and Cath hadn't finished their project. "Besides," she added quietly, "right now seems like a good time to be off-campus. Who knows what's going to happen here next?"

"You didn't have a very good time tonight, did you?" Quinn asked. Tobie had seemed withdrawn all evening. "Did you and Danny have a fight?"

Tobie shook her head. "No. He's a nice guy. It's just . . ." Her voice faded, and she sighed. "I guess I was just tired."

Tell me, Quinn urged silently, talk to me about what happened to you last year. You'll feel better, and maybe I can help.

But Tobie waved and left. There would be no discussion tonight.

When Quinn was in her own bed, she struggled to relax through her deep-breathing exercises, but it was impossible. The paint-stained sneakers and clothing hidden beneath her bed were screaming at her. What are you going to do about us? You can't just leave us here. Sooner or later, someone will spot us and want to know why your shoes and clothing have red paint splattered all over them. How will you explain, Quinn?

Chapter 9

The couple sat in a small car behind the tall, ivy-covered dorm.

It had just begun to rain, lightly at first, then more steadily. The windshield and windows were instantly covered with a thin sheen of wetness, as if they were sweating profusely. Later, the couple would say the rain was what kept them from seeing their attacker.

The figure moved slowly, deliberately, as if in a trance. It was shielded from the rain by a coat and hat. When it reached the small car, the right arm moved up, raising an object high above its head.

A claw hammer. Very large. Thick wooden handle, metal claw, dripping with raindrops.

The arm descended, swiftly and with great force, against the driver's door.

The couple inside, jolted back to reality by the blow, cried out.

The driver sat up straight, grabbed the door handle, pushed hard, even as another, harsher blow struck the door a second time, crumpling the metal and driving it inward, like a collapsing accordion.

The door wouldn't open.

The figure moved to the passenger's side and, while the driver was still trying to force open his own door, repeated the destruction on the passenger's door.

They were trapped.

The first blow to the windshield created a giant spiderweb of cracked glass.

The second blow, following immediately, partially shattered the cracked windshield, spraying the inside of the car with razor-sharp splinters. But much of the glass clung stubbornly to the windshield frame, forming small, jagged holes too small to crawl through unless the captives inside the car were willing to risk having a limb sliced away.

Thunder rumbled across the sky, drowning out the horrified cries of the car's occupants.

The left cheek of the girl in the passenger's seat was bleeding. She held one hand up to it, as if to hold her face together, her fear-stricken eyes fixated on the figure moving slowly around the car, hammer in hand.

The hammer struck again and again, this time attacking the windows.

Repeated blows to the windows brought a veined network of cracks. But the glass refused to give.

Both occupants of the car were bent double in the front seat, trying to protect their heads and faces.

Slam! against the driver's window. *Crash!* against the passenger's window. Shouting and screams from inside the car were drowned out by the wind and rain and thunder.

The figure moved back and forth in the downpour, giving up on the windows and slamming the hammer down upon the hood, then moving around to smash both headlights, then back to the driver's side to wield the weapon against the roof, over and over again.

Finally, with the passengers still cringing inside, the figure moved slowly away from the car and disappeared into the night.

Chapter 10

Quinn was rudely awakened by a commotion going on in the hall outside her room. People were shouting, feet were pounding along the hardwood floor. It sounded like horses stampeding.

She sat up. Rubbing her eyes sleepily, she switched on her table lamp and glanced at her alarm clock. Two o'clock. She hadn't been asleep that long.

What was going on?

"Tobie?"

Then she remembered. Tobie was spending the night at Nightmare Hall.

More shouting, more pounding feet . . .

Quinn slid out of bed, dragged a pair of jeans on over her T-shirt and loafers on over her socks, and stumbled to the door to open it.

Meg Pekoe, their resident advisor, was just passing.

"What's going on?" Quinn asked, her voice thick with sleep.

"Something's happened," Meg said breathlessly. "It was just on the campus radio. Come on, we're going out to see."

"See what?" Quinn's pulse was beginning to pound. Something bad . . . it was something bad, she could tell. But she hurried to the elevator with Meg. "What *is* it? What's happened?"

As Quinn and Meg moved into a crowded elevator, a girl from down the hall said, "The girl on the campus radio station said they just got a call that a couple was trapped in a smashed car out behind Lester. Not a car crash, though. She said the caller made it very clear that it hadn't been a car crash."

"If it wasn't a car wreck, what was it?" Meg asked. "How could a car be smashed if it wasn't in an accident?"

The girl shrugged. "Who knows? Maybe it's a joke. But the girl on the radio sounded really upset. She said it sounded to her like the couple was just sitting in their car and someone came up and smashed the car to pieces. Weird, right?"

A boy to Quinn's left nodded. "That's what I heard," he said. "That the doors were smashed in so they couldn't get out and then the rest of the car was attacked. Maybe with a hammer or an ax, sounds like."

"Who was it?" Quinn asked, "Whose car?"

"Don't know," came the answer. "No names. We'll find out when we get down there, I guess. Sounded like they were still inside the car. Trapped."

Quinn felt a little ghoulish. Should they really all be pouring out of the building to stare at two people trapped in a wrecked car and possibly injured? Creepy, when you thought about it.

But everyone knew the victims could be their friends. 'It was only natural that they'd be concerned.

The scene behind Lester was chaotic. A crowd had already gathered, and people were still arriving. Two police cars, their rooftop lights still revolving, sat off to one side, casting an eerie blue glow over the scene. Several officers were trying in vain to disperse the onlookers. If the storm hadn't passed, the crowd might have been smaller, but the skies had cleared and a full moon shone down upon the rain-slicked scene.

The car in question, she saw as she moved closer to the scene, was not one she recognized. Although there seemed to be a sea of glass on the ground surrounding the car, the spiderwebbed windows were still intact. Quinn could see two people sitting very close together in the front seat.

The glass on the ground had to have come from the windshield, now dotted with small holes with nasty-looking jagged edges. Both doors had caved inward under what must have been repeated blows with a heavy object.

There was hardly a square inch of space on the roof that hadn't been pocked with dents, like a golf ball.

"They're still in there," Suze said as Quinn arrived to join the group that included Ivy, Tim, and Danny. They all looked as stunned as Quinn felt. "The doors won't open," Suze continued. "The fire department is bringing the Jaws of Life. It's like a giant can opener. They'll have to cut the doors away."

The thought of people actually being inside that car while someone hammered blows down upon them sickened Quinn. How terrified they must have been!

"Whose car is that?" Quinn asked. "Who's in there?"

"Reed Combs and Jake Briggs. It's his car. They're both still in there."

"Oh, no," Quinn breathed. Reed and Jake. Another inseparable happy couple.

Chapter 11

While the fire fighters worked at removing the occupants of the car, the police officers examined the car and the area around it, looking for clues.

Quinn had never seen anyone look as bewildered as Reed when she was finally helped from the battered car. She was shaking so severely, she could hardly stand. A thin stream of red ran down one side of her face and the skin underneath it was ashen. Jake wasn't in much better shape. His eyes were dulled with shock as he surveyed the horrendous damage to his car.

Neither was able to hear normally, an aftereffect of the repeated clang of metal upon metal. Miraculously, they seemed to have only minor cuts and scratches. Nevertheless, they were quickly taken to the infirmary.

Simon showed up then. "Whoa," he said

when he saw the car, "Jake didn't make his car payment?" Then, seeing the look on Quinn's face, he said hastily, "Sorry. Bad joke. Anyone hurt?"

"Not physically," Suze said. "I guess they were <u>really</u> lucky."

"Obviously not an accident," Simon said. "Anyone know who did it?"

"No one on campus would have done this," Danny said firmly as the crowd began to disperse. "Had to be someone from off-campus."

"Off-campus?" Ivy said, her face very pale. "Danny, you're scaring me. Are you saying there's a stranger . . . a crazed one, at that . . . running around campus? Maybe armed with a sledgehammer or an ax?"

Danny shrugged. "Who knows? Doesn't do any good to panic, though. The police will handle it. They won't leave something like this in the hands of the security guards. They'll probably have the nut in custody by morning."

"Morning isn't that far away," Quinn pointed out wearily. "It took so long to get them out of that car." It was starting to rain again and now that the initial shock was over, Quinn realized how cold she was in her T-shirt.

"Here, take this," Simon said, removing his sweatshirt and handing it to her.

Quinn accepted gratefully and when she had

slipped the sweatshirt over her head, turned to face Simon. "Where were you? I thought you'd be out here with everyone else."

"Asleep," he answered. "No one woke me up. I'd still be pounding my pillow if it hadn't been for those sirens."

"Why are we hanging around here?" Ivy asked impatiently. Her sleek, dark hair was beginning to curl heavily from the dampness. "I hear my nice, cozy, warm bed calling to me. You guys coming?"

Quinn didn't want to leave. She wanted some answers about how and why this terrible thing had happened. But the police, the fire truck, and the crowd were leaving. There would be no answers tonight. It was time to leave.

With one last, worried look over her shoulder at the ruined car, she went with Ivy and Suze back to Devereaux.

Sleep was impossible. The sixth floor was alive with nervous activity. No one wanted to be alone to deal with their feelings or their fear. People gathered in friends' rooms to discuss what had happened, and then ran to other rooms to share theories about *why* it had happened. Doors slammed, feet pounded along the hall, and room 602 seemed to be one of the more popular places to gather.

As if *I* have the answer, Quinn thought, exhausted, as four more girls came into the room and joined the half dozen already sprawled on the floor. I was asleep when it happened. I don't know anything.

But she knew, too, that as tired as she was, sleeping now, when she was so upset, would be a major mistake. It could set off those hidden sensors that sent her wandering off into the night, unaware. That could *not* happen, not tonight with so many other people wandering the halls. Someone would see her, and then everyone on campus would be talking about Quinn Hadley. Only she wouldn't be plain old Quinn Hadley anymore, she'd be Quinn Hadley-the-Sleepwalker.

She wouldn't be able to stand that. That was why she'd sworn both Tobie and Simon to secrecy.

She settled back on her bed, leaning against the wall, listening to the theories.

The consensus, in spite of what Danny had said, seemed to be that the guilty party was someone on campus. The thought of a stranger among them, especially a criminally crazy stranger, was apparently a far more frightening idea.

"There's this geek in English class," Suze offered, "Joey-something. He's always had his eye on Reed. He's one of those quiet, broody types. Maybe he finally snapped."

A redhead named Chelsea from across the hall said, "Oh, Suze, Joey Bass wouldn't hurt a fly. I, personally, think it was someone from orchestra. Reed plays first violin. I play the viola and I can tell you, violinists are really jealous of each other. If Reed's hands had been cut by flying glass and she couldn't play, someone else would get her chair. That could be a really strong motive."

Quinn hadn't decided which was worse, thinking that one of their fellow students had suddenly flipped out and done all that damage, or thinking that some crazy stranger was roaming around loose on campus, armed with a hammer.

Looking thoroughly depressed, Ivy and Suze returned to their own room, and the gathering began to break up.

Suddenly, someone asked, "Geez, Quinn, you're not going to *sleep* in those, are you?"

Startled, Quinn looked at the speaker. It was Meg Pekoe, their RA, who had come to the door earlier to tell them to get back to bed, and then had changed her mind and stayed. Now, she was staring at Quinn's feet.

"What?" Quinn looked down. "Sleep in what?"

Meg wrinkled her nose. "Those *socks*!

They're filthy! Looks like you were running around outside in the rain in them. Didn't you take the time to stick a pair of shoes on your feet?"

"I had shoes on." She clearly remembered, when the commotion began out in the hall, slipping loafers on over her socks before she left the room, the same loafers that were now under her bed drying out. She also clearly remembered donning a fresh pair of clean white socks before she'd gone to bed. Her socks *couldn't* be dirty.

Everyone was staring at her feet.

Quinn bent her leg so she could study the bottoms of her white socks.

They were filthy. Black and gritty, as if she'd slogged through a coal mine without shoes.

"Oh, no," she whispered.

No one heard her.

"Oh, mine look like that all the time," Chelsea said. "I never wear shoes in the dorm, not even when I go down to do the laundry. What's the big deal?"

The big deal, Quinn thought, feeling nauseated, was that she had gone to bed wearing snowy white socks. When she'd left her bed during the uproar, she had immediately covered those socks with shoes. She had walked *nowhere* in her stocking feet. They couldn't possibly be dirty. But they *were*.

"Chelsea," Meg said, "you never got you socks *that* dirty walking around Devereaux. The floors aren't that disgusting. Quinn's socks look like she was running around outside."

"Meg," Quinn said, her voice cool, "Quit making such a fuss. You're embarrassing me." She was proud that her voice sounded so calm.

Dropping the subject, Meg went to the phone to call the infirmary and inquire about Reed and Jake.

She was smiling when she turned around. "They're both going to be okay," she said. "They're being released tomorrow morning." She glanced at her watch. "I mean, *this* morning. Listen, now that we know they're going to be okay, I've got to get some sleep. I'm out of here."

When she had gone and the others had followed, Quinn thought bleakly, The one thing I *don't* need is sleep. I can't risk it. At least I had a nap earlier. That'll have to hold me until morning.

She threw the ruined socks into the bathroom wastebasket and slipped on a clean pair. Then she went to the window and sat on the windowseat looking out until a gray, rainy dawn began to wash across campus.

Although she tipped her head back against

the windowframe and closed her eyes, she willed herself not to fall asleep.

Why were her socks so dirty? Had she been out of bed *before* Jake's car had been discovered? Had she been out of bed . . . in her *sleep*? If she had, where had she gone?

Quinn put her head in her hands. Why couldn't she *remember*? That was the worst part, not remembering. Sometimes she remembered bits and pieces . . . little things like the teddy bears on Sophie's shelves, staring at her with blank, glassy eyes as she bent over Sophie's bed. And the feel of branches brushing her cheek as she made her way through the woods to the cabin of her tennis rival. But she only remembered those things later, when someone had explained to her that she'd been walking in her sleep.

She hadn't left the dorm earlier, had she? Wouldn't she at least remember the rain on her face?

It was still raining when she decided to dress and go for a walk to clear her head. Tobie should be home soon. She had probably already heard about Reed and Jake. She'd have all kinds of questions.

But Quinn had no answers.

She dressed quickly and went to the closet for her yellow slicker and matching yellow rain hat. When she was a kid, she'd had a fit every time she'd had to wear an outfit exactly like it. Her mother had laughed when Quinn had come home from shopping for college and unearthed from a shopping bag the yellow rain gear. "*Now* you decide it's okay to wear," she'd said, "after all those arguments we had on rainy days!"

Quinn liked the brightness of the yellow and the slick, rubbery feel . . . exactly the same things she'd hated as a kid.

Well, she thought as she shrugged into the coat, that's what growing up is, I guess. Changing.

Slapping the hat on her head, she left the room.

The building was very quiet. Given the rainy, dreary weather and what had happened the night before, it seemed most people were sleeping in.

When the door to Devereaux had swung shut behind her, Quinn tilted her face upward, toward the rain, and slid her hands into the raincoat pockets.

And yelped softly, as something sharp sliced into a finger.

Quinn yanked her injured hand from the pocket. The ring finger on her left hand was bright red. A long, deep slice zigzagged its way up to the second knuckle.

What had she left in her pocket that was so sharp?

Pulling a tissue from her jeans pocket, she wrapped it around the bleeding finger and, using her other hand, hesitantly probed the depths of the left raincoat pocket.

Her fingers touched not one, but several sharp, jagged points.

Quinn stood perfectly still as her hand left that pocket and moved to the right one. Carefully, gingerly, her fingers tiptoed downward, until they touched . . .

Glass. Small pieces of sharp, jagged glass.

Her pockets were filled with broken glass.

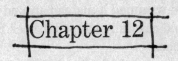

Chapter 12

Quinn stood in the rain in front of Devereaux, one hand in a pocket of the yellow slicker.

Why would there be broken glass in her raincoat pockets? How was that possible?

It wasn't.

But when she looked down at her left hand, the finger was still bleeding. Vivid red splotched the soggy tissue wrapped around it, as if to say to her, "It most certainly *is* possible, and here's the proof!"

Because she didn't know what else to do, she began walking. A few feet away from the door, she almost walked straight into a large trash container. She stopped, looking at it as if she'd never seen one before. Then her eyes cleared, and slowly, carefully, she began emptying her pockets, dropping each new shard of glass into the container as she unearthed it.

There wasn't that much of it. Half a dozen

pieces, like sand in the pockets of her shorts after she'd been to the beach.

She saved one thick, uneven splinter. Removing the bloody tissue from her wounded finger, she wrapped it instead around the piece of glass and carefully slipped it back inside the raincoat pocket.

Turning around, she headed for Lester.

Except for a few umbrella-sheltered teachers, briefcases in hand, dashing across campus, she had the early morning to herself. There was some comfort in that. She didn't want to run into anyone she knew, not now. She didn't trust herself to keep from blurting out, "I don't know where I was or what I did last night when I was supposed to be sleeping!"

When she reached Lester, she hesitated. She couldn't do it. Deliberately going back to take another look at that battered car was crazy. If she *had* been anywhere near the scene of the attack, she didn't want to know it. She *didn't*! What good would it do her? It would just make things worse than they already were.

But . . . hiding from the truth wouldn't do her any good, either, would it? If she had left the room last night, shouldn't she *know* it? If her nocturnal walks were becoming more frequent, she had to do something to stop them.

There had to be some way. Counseling or medication . . . tying herself to her bed, if necessary, anything to stop this feeling of having no control over her own life after she fell asleep.

Taking a deep breath and letting it out, Quinn rounded a corner of the building. Maybe the police had already removed the car, taking it away as evidence.

They hadn't. It was still there, sitting beside the building like a broken toy.

And someone was standing beside it. But it wasn't a policeman.

Involuntarily, Quinn took a step backward, into a narrow doorway. She didn't want to be seen approaching the car. Didn't the police always say a criminal was likely to return to "the scene of the crime"? If someone saw her there, they might think she'd had something to do with the attack.

Of course, she hadn't. She was just there to . . . to check something out, that was all.

But the same suspicion could apply to the person at the car now, couldn't it? What was he doing there, standing by the driver's side and reaching in through the yawning gap where the driver's door had been?

The rain came down harder, until she could barely see. But she didn't dare get any closer.

The figure, in jeans and a blue hooded jacket,

withdrew its arm. It was holding something in one hand. Then it straightened up and began to move away from the car. Walking quickly, shoulders hunched against the pelting rain, it hurried in Quinn's direction.

She did *not* want to be seen here.

Reaching behind her, she grabbed the door-knob and twisted. The door opened, and she darted inside, closing it quickly behind her.

But she stayed where she was, watching through the door's glass window. It seemed very important that she get a look at the person who had returned to the scene of the attack.

The window wasn't very clean. And the curtain of rain pulled a protective cloak around the tall figure, walking with its head down as it passed Lester.

But Quinn managed to get a good look as it passed only inches from where she stood.

Suze. The hood slid backward as she passed and Quinn could see her face clearly.

What was Suze doing at Jake's car?

If Quinn had had any doubt, the last of it disappeared as the figure reached the corner, and lifted its head before deciding which way to go. Quinn ducked further back into her hiding place, but that was Suze's face, all right.

When she was sure Suze was gone, Quinn darted back out into the rain and ran over to the car. The sea of broken glass surrounding the wreck was still there.

She carefully removed the large shard of tissue-wrapped glass from her raincoat pocket and, bending, picked up one of the larger pieces on the ground.

The two chunks of glass were exactly the same thickness.

They were exactly the same texture, fairly new, glossy-smooth.

They were exactly the same noncolor. No greenish tinge to one or pinkish tinge to another to differentiate them.

The two pieces of glass certainly looked identical.

Quinn stood up, feeling sick again. She dropped the telltale piece of glass on the ground, and hurried away from the car.

All thoughts of fresh air and exercise banished from her mind, she almost ran back to Devereaux.

When Quinn entered 602, Tobie's tote bag was lying on her bed. Good. Tobie had returned, but she was probably in the bathroom. There was time to do something about the raincoat. No one had seen her in it. If it *had* somehow been at the scene of the attack last night, she didn't want anyone knowing it was hers until she figured out exactly *how* it got there.

But putting it down the incinerator chute seemed like a bad idea. Suppose it *had* been seen behind Lester last night? If the police came around hunting for a yellow slicker and hat, she'd better be able to produce hers. A lot of people knew she owned a rain set like that. If she no longer had it, wouldn't the police wonder why?

She hadn't done anything wrong. Burning her raincoat would make her feel as if she had.

Instead, she rolled up the coat and hat in as small a ball as possible, wrapped them in an old sweatshirt, and placed them at the very back of the closet, behind a pile of dirty laundry. Even when the laundry was moved, all Tobie would see was an old sweatshirt.

Quinn felt almost as guilty as she would have if she'd burned the coat and hat.

Am I hiding evidence? she wondered as she wiped her face with a tissue and took clean, dry socks from a drawer.

Evidence of what? She hadn't *done* anything!

Suddenly, in her mind's eye, she saw herself raising her arms and lowering them, once, twice, three times, and then her younger sister Sophie's round, pink face screwed up in fear, her bright blue eyes wide with bewilderment as she woke from a sound sleep to find her beloved older sister pummeling her.

"But I didn't mean it!" Quinn whispered softly to herself, sinking down on the bed.

"What didn't you mean?" Tobie asked as she came into the room. Without waiting for an answer, she threw herself down on her bed. "I'm not leaving this room today," she said flatly. "It's lousy out there. I can afford to cut this one time. I'll get the notes from people. I'm just going to stay in bed."

"You okay?" Quinn asked. Tobie seemed awfully pale. Maybe she was scared. Who could blame her? That could just as easily have been her and Danny sitting in the car.

Tobie nodded and crawled back into bed.

It looked like a tempting idea. "It is getting pretty nasty out there."

"You were *outside*? Already? I thought you were probably downstairs eating breakfast. You don't have an eight o'clock on Fridays. What were you doing out there?"

Was Tobie deliberately avoiding the subject of last night's attack? She must have heard about it. How could they not talk about it? Impossible. "I just went for a walk, that's all. Listen, Tobie, is Suze a friend of Reed's? Or Jake's?"

Tobie's face fell. She'd heard about the attack, all right. She had obviously made up her mind to ignore it, pretend it hadn't happened.

But it had.

"Suze?" Tobie thought for a minute. "I don't know. Why?"

Quinn didn't want to tell Tobie that she'd seen Suze at the car. Not until she knew why Suze had been there. "I just wondered. Suze seemed really upset last night, so I thought . . ."

"I don't want to talk about this now," Tobie said, pulling her quilt up around her shoulders. She reached up and pulled her high school yearbook from the shelf. "And I'm sure Suze wasn't the only one upset about it. Everyone must be."

Yes, Quinn thought, but *everyone* didn't go back to the car at the crack of dawn this morning, did they?

Well, *two* of us did. I *know* why I was there. But why was Suze?

"Are you going to stay here with me?" Tobie asked, opening the yearbook.

Quinn shrugged. Maybe if she stayed inside, Tobie wouldn't bury herself in that yearbook again. It always seemed to depress her. On the other hand, Quinn wanted to get out on campus and find out what people were saying about last night's attack. "Count me out," she told Tobie. "I have a quiz in math, anyway. Can't afford to miss it."

When she left the room later, Tobie was lying on her bed looking at her yearbook, one hand reaching up to continually twist a lock of red hair.

Most of the gossip on campus revolved around the attack of the night before. Although Reed and Jake had been released from the infirmary that morning, they weren't attending classes. No one really expected them to.

But at lunch in Lester's busy cafeteria, Quinn was waiting on line for her soup when she overheard Suze and another girl, in line ahead of her, discussing the attack.

"Well, Reed _saw_ something," Suze told her companion.

Quinn moved an imperceptible inch forward. Reed had *seen* who attacked them? In all that rain?

"What?" the second girl said. "Did she see someone? Who was it?"

Quinn held her breath.

"Oh, she doesn't _know_ who," Suze replied. "All she knows is, it was someone wearing one of those yellow rubber raincoats and a matching hat."

Chapter 13

The day seemed to drag on endlessly. Quinn did all the things she was supposed to do: She went to class and she took notes, although she had no idea what she was writing.

She knew that she looked normal. Jeans and a sweater, normal. A little mascara on the thick eyelashes Tobie envied, normal. Straight brown hair fell around her face, normal. She walked like a normal person, sat like a normal person, probably even answered any questions put to her like a normal person.

But if people could have seen inside her head . . . a giant crazy quilt of questions spinning around in there like a load of colored clothes in a dryer. Reed had seen someone in a yellow raincoat and hat at the car. The pockets of the yellow raincoat in Quinn's closet had been full of glass. How had that glass made its way into her pockets? And what was Suze doing at the car first thing in the morning after the attack?

And . . . although it had nothing to do with the attack, why hadn't Tobie told her roomie about the boyfriend who had died? How could she *not* have told? Wouldn't keeping something so awful all to yourself be like carrying a mountain around on your shoulders?

Because it seemed important that she act as normal as possible, Quinn joined Ivy and Suze in a trip to the mall after classes. The rain had stopped, the sky had cleared, and the sun had warmed the air to bare-arm weather. It seemed the wrong kind of day to be sitting in an empty dorm room worrying over unanswered questions.

So she called Tobie from the lobby, inviting her along on the mall trip. "It's nice out now," she pleaded, "and you've been in that room all day. Come with us."

Tobie declined. She sounded tired, her voice husky.

She's been crying, Quinn thought with certainty. I should hide that yearbook from her. It just makes her sad.

Giving up, she joined Ivy and Suze out on the Commons.

"No gloomy talk about attacks on innocent, helpless cars," Ivy half-joked on the way to the mall. "I'm as upset about it as you are, but it's too nice a day to try to analyze why some crazy with a hammer would go after a helpless sedan, okay?"

"Okay with me," Quinn said as she steered her own small blue compact car around a curve. Ivy had a point. Why waste time discussing a puzzle when no one had the missing pieces? Maybe this day could still be salvaged. And maybe she'd get the chance to ask Suze what she was doing at Jake's car that morning.

They did have fun. Suze bought two new pairs of outrageously expensive earrings, Ivy found a CD she'd been hunting for for weeks, and Quinn tested four or five shades of lipstick, one a bold, daring red, which she didn't buy. No guts, she accused silently, buying instead a pale coral shade.

Suze drove Ivy and Quinn crazy, stopping every few minutes to talk to a different guy.

"She is the most incredible flirt I've ever seen!" Ivy said with some disgust.

Quinn laughed. "Look who's talking."

Ivy shrugged. "Yeah, but it's just a game to me. You don't see me latching on to any one guy, do you? Who needs it?"

"Does Tim know you feel that way? He looks to me like he has great expectations concerning the two of you."

"Tim's okay. But I'm still having fun . . ."

Ivy was as casual about Tim, who seemed nuts about her, as Tobie was about Danny.

"I guess you and Simon are sailing along smoothly now," Ivy said, stopping to gaze into a sporting goods store window. "Don't you think that's kind of risky?"

"Risky? Risky how?"

"Well," Ivy turned away from the window, "some of the couples on campus aren't going out in public now. They're afraid to. I guess they think being a twosome on campus right now is a dangerous thing."

Quinn wanted to retort that people were just being silly, but the words stuck in her throat. Because maybe they weren't. The attacks had all been on couples. How could you ignore that?

Ignoring it might be . . . what was the word Ivy had used . . . dangerous?

"I need new sneakers," she said, pulling Ivy into the sporting goods store. She did need new sneakers, although she hated the thought of *why* she needed them. Not to mention new white socks, she thought dismally.

She was at the sock rack when Suze caught up with her. Quinn turned around when Suze said her name. Ivy was at the rear of the store, trying on boots. It seemed like the perfect time to ask Suze what she was doing at Jake's car this morning.

But, Quinn thought, then she'll want to know what *I* was doing there.

So, I'll fib.

Blonde hair up in a curly ponytail, blue eyes wide with pleasure as she joined Quinn, Suze looked like the most innocent person in the world. "Suze," Quinn began, "have you heard any more about Reed and Jake? I can't believe they got out of that car with only some scratches, can you?"

"No, but they did. I saw Reed this morning. She had a Band-Aid on one cheek and some scratches on her hands, but that's all. They were really lucky."

"I'll say." Quinn fingered a pair of thick white socks and said very casually, "I wandered over to the car this morning to see what was left of it in daylight, and I thought I saw you there."

"You did? I didn't see you."

Quinn felt her cheeks grow warm. That's because I was hiding, Susan, like the sneaky person that I am. Aloud, she said, "No? So . . . what were you doing there?"

"I was getting something for Reed," Suze answered without hesitation. "She called early this morning, said she'd left her purse on the front seat."

Ivy joined them then, and Quinn dropped the matter. Who was she to be grilling Suze?

Hadn't she herself been at the car? And which of the two of them was Most Likely To Be Suspected? Which one of them had found a paint-stained skirt and sweater in her room? Which one had been wearing grungy, grimy socks in bed shortly after the attack on Jake's car, and which one had found glass fragments in her raincoat pockets?

And which one sleepwalked, wandering around at night like some beady-eyed nocturnal animal when everyone else was asleep?

Not Suze.

Maybe it was time for Quinn Hadley to visit a campus counselor again. She didn't want to. Talking with a counselor would make her feel like she was really losing it.

Well, maybe she was.

They stopped at Vinnie's on the way home. To Quinn's surprise, Reed and Jake were there, sitting quietly in a corner booth. The simple Band-Aid on Reed's cheek lied about the severity of the attack.

"I didn't expect to see *them* here," Suze commented. "You'd think after their narrow escape, they'd be hiding in their rooms." She shook her head and her ponytail bounced. "It's a miracle that they weren't hurt worse than they were."

"They must have ducked the first time the

hammer hit the car," Ivy commented, reaching for a napkin. "Or maybe they both fainted, face-down. I know I would have."

"Me, too," Quinn agreed. In her mind's eye, she saw a yellow-clad figure lifting a large hammer, slamming it down against the car . . .

"I'm not hungry," she announced, standing up. "Just order me something to drink, okay? I'll be right back."

She hurried over to the table in the corner. "I'm glad you guys aren't lying in hospital beds," she told Reed and Jake. "We were just talking about how lucky you were. I mean," she added hastily, "I'm sure it was horrible, but it could have been so much worse."

Reed nodded. "We know, Quinn. Of course, Jake here is without wheels now."

Quinn couldn't help noticing that Reed's hand shook slightly as she lifted her glass.

Small wonder.

"Well, at least no one stole your purse from the car," she said to Reed. "It would have been so easy to just reach in through that broken windshield and yank it right out of there."

Reed looked up at Quinn. "My purse?"

Quinn nodded. "I'm not surprised that you forgot it when the fire fighters helped you out of there. You must have been so glad to get free."

"I didn't forget my purse, Quinn. What are you talking about?"

Quinn's eyes moved from Reed's face to Suze, standing over by the jukebox, flirting outrageously with "Mower" Platte, one of the football players.

She lied, Quinn thought. She *lied*.

Well, her conscience snickered, *you* were going to lie to *her*, if you had to. You just didn't have to, that's the only difference between the two of you.

I *know* why I was going to fib, Quinn thought. Because that raincoat and hat are lying in the back of my closet. But why did Suze lie?

Quinn made up a flimsy excuse for commenting about Reed's purse, and returned to the booth, where she announced that she wanted to leave. Headache.

No one argued.

When they got back to campus, Quinn went straight to the library, where she staked out a quiet corner and tried to decide what to do. She needed to talk to someone about all of this. Simon? Maybe. She was seeing him later. But she hated to dump all of this on him when they'd just made up. They weren't that sure of each other yet.

Ivy? Suze was Ivy's roommate, and a good

friend. Ivy knew Suze was a flirt, but she probably wouldn't even consider the idea that Suze could be something worse.

And Tobie had problems of her own. It didn't seem fair to overload her.

There didn't seem to be a whole lot of choice, and Quinn *had* to talk to someone.

Sighing, she got up and left the library, walking directly to the student services offices at Butler Hall, the administration building.

If she absolutely *had* to talk to someone, it might as well be the counselor she'd talked with before. At least she wouldn't have to start from scratch. The thought of starting from the very beginning was mind-boggling.

Oh, that's pretty funny, she thought as she pulled the heavy wooden door open. Like my mind isn't already boggled to the max. Maybe even beyond repair.

She was just about to turn a corner when she heard a familiar voice say an even more familiar name. She stopped, remaining safely behind the corner wall.

"Stop in any time, Tabitha. I'm always here for you, you know that. You mustn't keep things bottled up inside. It's not healthy. It can be dangerous. And Tabitha," said the voice softly, "time really does heal even the worst pain. I promise."

The voice that answered quietly, "Thanks a lot, Doctor. See you next week," was even more recognizable.

Quinn shrank back against the wall, making herself as small as possible, then breathed a sigh of relief as the footsteps turned in a different direction and faded.

The voice belonged to her counselor, the one she had confessed to about her sleepwalking. The therapist had said almost the same thing to Quinn. "It'll get better, Quinn, I promise." A very optimistic woman.

The footsteps belonged to Tabitha.

How many Tabithas could there be on campus? And if there *was* another, it wouldn't have that voice, would it? The voice that belonged to Tabitha Thomason.

Tabitha Thomason, better known to friends and family as Tobie.

Her roommate Tobie.

It wasn't so surprising, after what Quinn had learned about Tobie recently, that her roommate was seeing a counselor. For that matter, even without the horrendous event in Tobie's past, she could easily have been seeing a counselor because she was homesick, or having a hard time with her studies.

Lots of people on campus probably talked with the counselors. *I* was on my way to see one, Quinn told herself. Why shouldn't Tobie?

Right. Why *shouldn't* Tobie?

It was at that precise moment that Quinn remembered where she'd seen the bright pink paper like the sheet that Simon had pulled from his wallet.

On Tobie's cork bulletin board over her desk.

Tobie often had trouble concentrating, remembering things, and so she often wrote notes to herself about her schedule or library books to be returned or assignments to finish. She pushpinned the notes to her bulletin board and discarded them when they were no longer needed.

The pushpins, Quinn remembered, were yellow.

But the notes were pink. Bright pink. Each and every one of them was the same exact color and texture as the piece of paper telling Simon Kent that Quinn Hadley wasn't interested in having him in her life anymore.

The letter to Simon had been written on Tobie's stationery.

Chapter 14

Tobie wasn't in the room when Quinn got back, but she had left a note on her bulletin board. *Not* on pink stationery but on plain white notepaper.

Went over to Danny's, Quinn read. *Back later. Have fun with Simon.*

So, Tobie had finally decided to get out of her funk. Talking with the counselor must have made her feel better.

There were no pieces of bright pink stationery pushpinned to the bulletin board. The other two notes, one a laundry reminder, the other a scribbled phone number, were both on plain white notepaper.

Had Tobie run out of bright pink? Or . . . didn't want to use it for fear Simon had shared his letter with Quinn (as he *had*) and Quinn would recognize the paper?

The first moment they were in this room

together, just the two of them, Tobie was going to have to explain that letter.

Pushing the unpleasant matter from her mind, Quinn took a quick shower and got ready for her date with Simon. They were driving into Twin Falls for dinner at Hunan Manor, Quinn's favorite place to eat, and then taking in a movie. Just the two of them. Quinn's idea. She had decided they needed to get reacquainted, and that would be easier without a crowd around.

Ivy had pretended to be insulted. "You're not coming to Tim's frat party? Okay, that does it, Quinnie, you are no longer in my will."

Quinn laughed. "You don't have any money, Ivy."

"That's not the point." Ivy, in a thick white bathrobe, hair turbanned in a white towel, was sprawled across Tobie's bed. "It's the thought that counts. Come on, Quinn, the party's going to be a blast. It's bad enough that Tobie wimped out. Now you're telling me neither of my best friends is going to be at this festive celebration?"

"Suze is going, isn't she? I thought *she* was your best friend." Maybe she wouldn't be, Quinn thought, if you knew that she lies. "Besides," she added dolefully, "what is there to celebrate with all the creepy things happening on this campus."

"You're *all* my best friends," Ivy said. "And Tim said we're having this party to show that we're not afraid. Thumb our nose at that maniac, so to speak."

"There's bravery and then there's stupidity," Quinn pointed out.

"Look who's talking. You and Simon are going out *alone*, as a *couple*, while the rest of us are going to be hanging out together. Not even a crazy person would be dumb enough to descend on a crowded frat house. But this particular crazy doesn't seem to have any problem at all attacking a couple. That's you and Simon, Quinn."

"I need to be alone with him," Quinn insisted. "We have some things to straighten out. Maybe we'll drop by the party later."

Ivy seemed satisfied with that, and left to get dressed, adding that if Quinn showed up at the party, she just might consider putting her back in the will.

Quinn was laughing as the door closed.

But the uneasiness had returned. Ivy could be right. Maybe it was foolish to go out as a lone couple on this particular Friday night. Were she and Simon just asking for trouble?

Well, that depends, a niggling little voice

said, on who's doing these nasties. Are you forgetting it *could* be you? You'd hardly attack *yourself*, would you?

Oh, I don't know, Quinn thought drily. Seems to me, if I'm crazy enough to set off a stink bomb, pour paint on people, and attack a car with a hammer, I'm probably crazy enough to do almost anything.

They did *not* talk about the incidents on campus at dinner. Quinn was surprised to discover that no one else from campus was in the small Chinese restaurant. Although it wasn't as popular with students as Vinnie's or Burgers Etc., there were usually a handful of couples from Salem at the round, white-covered tables on a weekend night.

But not this weekend night.

"I wonder where everyone is?" she mused aloud.

"Probably at the frat party," Simon answered, wielding chopsticks as if he'd been born with a pair in his fingers. "We can check it out after the movie if you want."

They talked about life at college throughout dinner. It was a challenge to tackle that subject without mentioning what life at their particular college had become recently, but Quinn noticed gratefully that Simon was as determined as she was to avoid such an unpleasant topic. He talked about prelaw, she about science, and after a while they became so caught up in their discussion that the recent attacks slid onto a back burner and stayed there.

The movie was less satisfying. A bittersweet romance, it ended unhappily, leaving a sour taste in Quinn's mouth as they left the theater. "Tobie and Ivy would have loved it," she said as they headed back to campus. "I can just hear both of them, saying, 'Well, Quinn, what did we tell you? Nothing ever lasts!' "

Simon reached over and took her hand in his, driving one-handed. "Well," he said with a grin, "now that we've straightened things out, it'll be fun proving them wrong, won't it?"

Satisfied with that, Quinn settled back in her seat for the ride to campus.

"So," Simon said as they made the turn off the highway and onto the wide driveway leading between the dorms, "feel like checking out Tim's frat party?"

"Yeah, I'd like to see if Danny and Tobie showed up," Quinn replied. "She hasn't been in much of a party mood lately, but Danny is a friend of Tim's, so maybe he talked her into it. Tobie could use a good party."

But, they discovered when they walked into the huge white house, if a "good party" was what they were looking for, they weren't going to find it at Sigma Chi. Not on this Friday night.

"Where is everyone?" Quinn asked Ivy, who came to greet them. "This place is deader than a cemetery." There were only half a dozen couples in the massive living room, sitting glumly on plaid couches, there was no music playing, and the only conversation seemed to be a tall, blonde girl complaining repeatedly that she was bored.

"No one showed," Ivy explained, handing Quinn and Simon each a filled paper cup. "Can you believe it? Everyone I talked to on campus last week was looking forward to this party."

She led them over to the fireplace, where they all sat on the raised stone hearth. "If you're thinking that you got here too late to be a part of the crowd, forget it. It never got any bigger than this," waving her hand to encircle the couples lounging on the couches. "They've got enough food left to feed all of campus for a week. What a waste!"

"Were Danny and Tobie here?" Quinn asked.

"Quinn, you're not listening to me! I said, this is *it*. No one else came. Not Danny, not Tobie, not most of campus. People are scared." Ivy shook her head. "It's funny, I thought you and Simon were dumb for going out together as a couple. I thought people would feel safer here, in a crowd. Apparently, no one else agreed."

Simon leaned forward, across Quinn, to address a question to Ivy. "You think no one showed because they're scared?"

"Well, of *course*. A lot of people come to these parties with a date. But no one *wants* to be seen as a couple these days. They figure that makes them a target." Ivy sighed heavily. "I guess I can't blame them. I wish the police would come up with something, put an end to all this craziness. If this keeps up, there is going to be absolutely no social life *left* on this campus."

Quinn and Simon saw no point in staying, and, in fact, before they took their leave, three other couples left.

The expressions on Tim's and Ivy's faces as Quinn and Simon left were desolate.

"I feel so sorry for Tim and his frat brothers," Quinn told Simon as they walked to Devereaux. "I've always wondered what would happen if you gave a party and nobody came. Now I know. Grim. Very grim. And it's not as if it's their fault."

Simon shrugged. "I don't know, maybe they should have figured. I mean, you can't blame people for being a little jumpy, right?"

"Are *you* nervous?" Quinn asked. "I mean, about the two of us being out here alone?" It hadn't occurred to her that Simon might be at all rattled. He seemed so calm, so cool.

Simon laughed. "Well, let's just say I'm not kissing you good night on the front steps of Devereaux. There could be someone on the roof armed with water balloons or, worse, another stink bomb. We'll say good night at the door to your room, okay? And I think it might be a good idea to hike up six flights of stairs and avoid the elevator. Call me paranoid, but where do you run if you're threatened by some maniac in an elevator?"

Quinn knew he was just being careful, but somehow the knowledge that someone as levelheaded as Simon was feeling cautious just made her more nervous.

She wondered what Simon would say if she told him about the smelly red jacket, the raincoat's pockets, the blouse and skirt still balled up under her bed. She should tell him. He had said in the car that they were going to "last." How could they last if she kept things hidden from him?

But . . . if she told him and he thought she'd had anything to do with the attacks, they wouldn't last at all, would they? How could

Simon love someone who'd done what she might have done?

She couldn't tell him. She couldn't. Not yet.

She couldn't tell him the truth until she knew what the truth *was*.

Chapter 15

The two were seated on the low stone wall surrounding the fountain on the Commons. Darkness had fallen, and campus was deserted. Couples who ordinarily would be meandering across campus hand-in-hand or lounging on one of the tower terraces or saying good night in parked cars had taken to giving up those activities. It no longer seemed safe.

It had turned suddenly chilly, and they huddled together for warmth, reluctant to end the evening.

They saw no one approaching, and in fact had commented on how empty and desolate campus seemed. They heard nothing but the sound of the few remaining leaves rippled by a gusty wind.

The hammer, when it hit, came soundlessly, with no more than a whisper as it descended, and descended again.

The attack was so swift, so sure, that neither made a sound as first he, and then she, toppled off the wall and onto the ground.

On the deserted late-night campus, no one saw the figure, hammer in hand, moving slowly away from the scene, as if in a trance.

Chapter 16

Before Quinn told Simon good night, she asked him for the letter. He didn't ask why she wanted it. He handed her the pink sheet of paper without comment, and kissed her good night.

Anxious to confront Tobie, Quinn hurried upstairs to their room, hoping her roommate would be home.

She was. Tobie was sitting up in bed, and Quinn knew she'd been crying again. Her eyes were swollen and red-rimmed.

Quinn hesitated. This seemed like a terrible time to accuse Tobie of something. But she *had* to know. And . . . would there ever be a *good* time?

Silently, she held out the sheet of paper.

Tobie looked at it with her swollen eyes. "What?" she said thickly. "What's that?"

Quinn pushed the letter at her. "Read it!"

Then she went over and sat down on her bed.

Tobie read quickly. She lifted her head. "You wrote this? I thought you two were back together."

"*I* didn't write that," Quinn said sharply. She glanced pointedly at Tobie's typewriter, sitting amid a mass of clutter on Tobie's desk. "Someone else wrote it. Recognize the paper?"

Tobie looked blank for a second. "The paper? No . . . oh, well, I guess it's like mine . . ." her voice trailed off and then her eyes opened wider. She stared at Quinn. "You don't . . . you mean . . . you think *I wrote this*?" Fresh tears gathered in her eyes. "Quinn! I wouldn't! Why would I?" —never in my life.. "

Quinn shrugged. "Maybe because Simon and I were happy and you hated that? Because you aren't? Or maybe you were just worried about me. I mean, with your attitude about romance, maybe you didn't want me to get hurt. How should *I* know why you did it?"

Tobie sat up very straight. "But I didn't! Quinn, I swear, I didn't write this!" The tears spilled down over her cheeks. "I can't believe you'd think I'd deliberately sabotage what you had going with Simon. You must think I'm a terrible person."

Quinn relented. "No, I don't think that, Tobie. But I do think you're really unhappy. Because . . ." She had to say it *sometime*. "Because of what happened to you."

Every last ounce of color drained from Tobie's face. "What?" she whispered. "What are you talking about?"

Quinn sank back against the wall beside her bed. "I *know*, Tobie. Tim told me. I know that someone you loved died last year. I wish *you* had told me. It would have explained a lot. It explains a lot *now*, but I'd rather it had come from you."

"You're wrong," Tobie said softly. "It doesn't explain what you think it does, because I did *not* write that letter to Simon. Someone else did, on my stationery. And I'm sorry I didn't tell you about Peter."

"Peter?"

"Peter Gallagher. Peter John Gallagher, the one love of my life. I know that sounds corny, Quinn, but it's true. I couldn't tell you about him because I knew if I tried, I'd end up bawling, and then you'd feel sorry for me. I don't want sympathy, Quinn. I don't want to be pitied. I came here to make a new start, and I couldn't do that if everyone knew and felt sorry for me. Coming to Salem was what Peter and I had planned. So, even though what I really wanted to do was crawl into bed and stay there, I decided to come. I knew he'd want me to."

Quinn sat silently for a moment, and then said, "Can't you tell me about it now, Tobie? You shouldn't be carrying around something so awful all by yourself. No wonder you're so depressed."

Tobie didn't answer right away. She gnawed on a fingernail, her eyes closed, and then she said, "You're right. If you'll turn off the lights, I'll tell you. It'll be easier that way. I don't want to see you looking at me with big, sad eyes."

Quinn got up and turned off the lights. Then she returned to her own bed and settled against the wall again.

Tobie sighed heavily. Her voice, when it came out of the darkness, was soft but steady. "We'd gone to a Christmas dance. We went out to dinner first, at a really expensive hotel in town, and Peter had spent too much money. So, on the way home from the dance, he wanted to stop at one of those automatic bank teller machines. I told him it could wait until morning. It was late and I was tired. But Peter insisted. So he found a machine, and we stopped."

Quinn listened silently. A bank teller machine? What did that have to do with how Peter Gallagher had died?

"I stayed in the car," Tobie continued, her

voice eerily calm in the darkened room. "It was very late, and the machine only had this one tiny little light. So I didn't get out of the car." Her voice rose suddenly. "I *didn't* get out of the car! If I had . . ."

"What happened?" Quinn pressed, knowing that if she let Tobie quit now, she'd never hear the whole story.

A deep breath from the other side of the room. Then, "The guy came out of nowhere. I didn't see him coming, and I know Peter didn't, either, or he would have turned around. He was facing the machine, and all of a sudden there was this guy in grungy clothes, standing right behind Peter, saying something. I couldn't hear what he was saying, but I knew when Peter turned around and I saw the look on his face, that there was something really wrong. I rolled my window down partway so I could hear. Peter said, "No, I'm not giving you anything." He was so stubborn. I loved that about him . . ." Tobie's voice broke, and when she spoke again, Quinn could hear tears. . . . "but that's what killed him. It *killed* him!"

"He was being robbed?" Quinn asked, disbelief in her voice.

"Yes. It happens a lot at those machines, I heard later, especially at night. But we didn't know that. At least, I didn't. Anyway, Peter wouldn't let the guy have any money. The guy got really mad and pulled something out of his pocket. It was a gun. I almost died, I was so scared for Peter."

"He was shot?" Quinn felt like she'd strayed into a detective show on television. This couldn't really have happened, could it? To Tobie? A robbery? A gun?

"No. We didn't know it then, but the gun was a fake. It looked incredibly real, though. I guess Peter panicked, because he made a grab for the gun, the guy tried to push him away, and Peter lost his balance and fell. He hit his head on the cement at the base of the machine." Tobie was crying openly now. "That's what killed him. The fall. But," her voice hardened, "it wouldn't have happened if the robber hadn't been there. It was *his* fault!"

"Of course it was." Quinn struggled to accept as reality what seemed so bizarre, so unreal. "Tobie, I'm so sorry. It must have been horrible."

"You can turn the light back on now," Tobie whispered. "I need to find a tissue."

Quinn had just flipped the switch and flooded the room with light when a sharp rapping sounded on the door.

"Not now!" she called, thinking it was someone wanting to borrow shampoo or a hair dryer. "We're busy."

"It's Meg Pekoe," their RA's voice said, "let me in! Something's happened! Hurry!"

Quinn yanked the door open.

Meg was standing in the hall, supporting Ivy. Ivy had one hand to the back of her head, her eyes half-closed. When she took her hand away, it was bright red.

"I found her out here in the hall," Meg said. "She doesn't know where she is or what she's doing, and she's bleeding. It's her head. Help me get her to a bed."

"Tim," Ivy murmured, "Tim's still out there. By the fountain. He's hurt. . . ." then her eyes closed all the way and her knees buckled.

Chapter 17

With a dazed Ivy lying on Quinn's bed, Tobie rushed into the bathroom to wet a washcloth, Quinn left to give Suze the bad news, and Meg ran to get a security guard to help her look for Tim.

She came back an hour later, after Ivy had been taken to the infirmary, to tell Tobie and Quinn that Tim had been found, lying on the ground beside the fountain. He was unconscious, and hadn't revived by the time Meg left the infirmary. Suze had opted to stay there until a distraught Ivy had fallen asleep.

"Ivy said they didn't see or hear anything," Meg said wearily, leaning against the door. "We don't know any more than we did before."

But Quinn did. For the first time since the attacks had started, she knew positively that she'd had nothing to do with this one. She hadn't been asleep this time.

And . . . if she hadn't had anything to do with *this* attack . . . then didn't it seem likely that she hadn't had anything to do with the others, either?

But there was the matter of the red jacket that smelled of rotten eggs. And the raincoat . . . the glass in the pockets . . . and the paint-stained skirt and blouse and shoes. What about those? She couldn't just ignore them.

Quinn, a rational voice inside her head said sternly, *anyone* could have put those things in your room. *Anyone.*

Why hadn't the thought occurred to her before? She'd been so frightened . . . so scared that she'd been doing terrible things in her sleep. Why had it never crossed her mind that someone might be trying to make her *think* she'd done those things?

Because the idea was so crazy.

Who would do something like that? And why? Why would someone want her to think she was doing maniacal things?

Cruel. That was so cruel. Almost as bad as the attacks themselves.

But then, someone who would strike another human being's skull with a hammer wouldn't balk at pinning his crimes on someone else, would he?

An emotionally exhausted Tobie had fallen

sound asleep shortly after Ivy had been taken away. She lay sprawled across the narrow bed, one hand tangled in her mop of red hair.

A wave of sympathy washed over Quinn. Tobie had already been through so much, and now this . . .

The question now was, she thought as she sat at her desk and turned on the lamp, how many people on campus knew she was a sleepwalker? Had there been other people out in the hall that first night? She hadn't asked Tobie, but there could have been. For that matter, Simon or Tobie might have accidentally let it slip. Or they could have been discussing it somewhere on campus and been overheard.

She would ask Tobie tomorrow if she had told anyone about her nocturnal habits. Because it seemed painfully clear that her sleepwalking was what made her a target for framing.

The following morning Quinn decided to look for Suze. It was time to find out exactly why Suze had lied to her about fishing Reed's purse from the wrecked car. What would make Suze lie about something like that?

As Quinn went into the bathroom to shower, it occurred to her that Suze might know she sleepwalked. Tobie might have told her, maybe thinking that Quinn needed more than one keeper, in case Tobie wasn't around one night. And Suze knew which room was Quinn's, knew she owned the yellow raincoat, could have come and gone when no one was home. They didn't always lock their door. In fact, they hardly ever locked it. They'd never seen any reason to lock it.

But then, not only had they not expected anyone at Devereaux to come in and *steal* things, they certainly hadn't expected anyone to come in and *hide* things.

Suze? It was hard to imagine her doing something as vicious as slugging someone over the head with a hammer.

Well, hey, it was hard to imagine *anyone* doing something so awful. And almost impossible to think it could be someone she *knew*.

But, of course, it *had* to be someone she knew. Or someone who knew *her*. And, in fact, knew a lot about her. Knew that she had a hard time staying in bed at night.

After her shower, Quinn couldn't find the hair dryer. Tobie often borrowed it — and like everything else, she rarely put it back.

Muttering to herself, Quinn began to hunt. It was too cold to go outside with wet hair. She'd freeze. Where had Tobie *put* the stupid dryer?

She checked around Tobie's dresser and night table, which were covered with a jumble of tissues, books, pens, and other stuff, but no hair dryer.

Impatient and very annoyed, Quinn looked around Tobie's unmade bed. When she crouched down and peered underneath, she didn't really expect to find the hair dryer. Even someone as careless as Tobie probably wouldn't have tossed a hair dryer under a bed.

And the hair dryer wasn't under there.

But the hammer *was*.

Chapter 18

Quinn knelt beside the bed and stared at the hammer as if it were a reptile about to strike. From where she knelt, she could clearly see the rusty stains on the claw. Blood . . .

She sank back on her heels. It had happened again. Something used in an attack on campus had made its way into her room.

But this time, it wasn't under *her* bed.

It was under Tobie's bed. Tobie . . . who had been so shattered by Peter Gallagher's death that she was still seeing a counselor. Unhappy Tobie . . .

How unhappy?

It would have been so easy for Tobie to plant all those things in their room.

The thought made Quinn sick. But if not letting anger out could make someone walk in their sleep and punch out a sister and wreck a tennis racket, maybe a broken heart could do the same kind of thing. Maybe Tobie didn't really *know* what she was doing. Or couldn't help it. Maybe that's why she was seeing a counselor.

Had Tobie really been with Danny all of last evening?

Hating herself, Quinn got up and went to the telephone to call Danny's frat house. When he was on the line, she said, "Danny, it's Quinn. Tobie's in the shower, but she wanted me to call and ask if you'd happened to find her wallet. She thought she might have dropped it when you guys were out last night."

"You mean Thursday night," Danny said.

"No . . . I thought she said last night."

"I didn't see Tobie last night. She holed up in her room all day yesterday. Said she felt lousy. I'll check my car, though, see if she left it there Thursday night."

Quinn hung up. Tobie had lied about being with Danny last night.

Why?

She couldn't keep wrestling with this thing on her own. The attack on Tim and Ivy had been the worst one yet. Playing amateur detective wasn't going to solve anything.

Making up her mind, Quinn gathered together the raincoat, the skirt and blouse and paint-stained sneakers, and gingerly toed the hammer out from underneath the bed with one foot, being careful to wrap a tissue around her hand before she picked it up and stuffed it into a plastic bag with the other items.

Then she left the building and drove to town, straight to the police station.

"I found these in my room on campus," she told the officer she'd been directed to. "I thought you should have them."

The policeman was big, with a thick crop of graying hair and a friendly smile. The smile disappeared when she emptied the plastic bag out upon his desk, which was littered with newspaper articles and manila folders.

They talked for nearly an hour, and when she had finished answering his questions, he seemed convinced that she had no idea how the raincoat had gathered its glass, how the skirt, blouse, and shoes had collected paint stains, or how the hammer had ended up under her room-mate's bed.

"I'll just keep these," he said, stuffing the items back into their bag. "Should be a lot of help." He fixed intelligent eyes on Quinn. "Might be a good idea if you didn't say anything to anyone about coming here, okay?"

Quinn nodded. She understood.

She was about to leave when she glanced

down at the desk, the surface now free of her things, and gasped.

A picture of Tobie Thomason was staring back up at her from a newspaper clipping.

The caption beneath the photo read :

GIRL TESTIFIES AGAINST
BOYFRIEND'S ATTACKER

well read it Girl.

"What . . . what is that?" Quinn managed, one shaky finger pointing toward the desk.

The policeman's eyes followed Quinn's finger. "You know her?"

"She's . . . she's my roommate. Why do you have that clipping on your desk? Can I read it?"

"I can tell you what it says. Your roommate," he tapped the photo with a finger, "sent a real sleaze bag to prison for a very long time. Name of Gunther Brach. He decided to help himself to someone else's funds. Tried to take it from this girl's boyfriend, Peter Gallagher."

Quinn nodded. "I know about that. But I didn't know Tobie testified."

"It's not our case," the officer said. "Happened over in Riverdale. But when all this stuff started on campus, the Thomason girl's parents gave us a call. They were worried about her.

Testifying was real hard on the girl. Got a lot of death threats by phone and mail before the trial. Could have backed out, but she didn't. The force in Riverdale thinks there was someone else in the car with Brach that night, someone who didn't want Miss Thomason to testify. By the time they picked the guy up after the robbery, he was alone, and insisted he'd been alone all night. But they figure he took his accomplice home before they caught up with him."

"Do you have any idea who that was? With him when he did it, I mean?"

The policeman shook his head. "Could have been a pal, a girlfriend, who knows? Brach wasn't talking. Honor among thieves, that kind of thing, I guess. He wasn't going to rat on a friend. I talked to one of the officers on the case. Apparently, there were a couple of possibles in court every day. A heavyset blonde girl who stared daggers at Thomason while she was testifying, and a couple of young fellows looked like they might be friends of Brach's.

"But they never got anything concrete on any of them, and, like I said, Brach wasn't talking."

"And Tobie's parents are worried now?" Quinn couldn't blame them. If all the parents knew what was happening on campus, the student body would be yanked out of Salem so fast, the dorms would empty like sinking ships.

"The girl . . . your roommate . . . did a real fine job of testifying. Brach was convicted and hauled off to prison. But according to her parents, once that was over, the girl fell apart. Really went to pieces. I guess it's no secret that she had to be hospitalized. They were real open and honest about it, so I guess since you're her roommate, you probably know all about it."

No. No, I didn't know, Quinn thought sadly.

"Can't blame the poor kid," the officer went on. "Watching her boyfriend die, then being scared to death by threats, and then having to testify in open court. Took a lot of guts to get up there on the stand. She okay now?"

Good question. *Was* Tobie okay? Or had the horror of watching Peter Gallagher die and the death threats afterward and the testifying done far more damage to her mind than anyone suspected? Had her stay in the hospital worked? Or not?

"Yes," Quinn said, "she's fine. We're all upset by what's happening on campus, though. I wonder, do you know the names of those people who came to the trial every day? The blonde girl, and the two guys?"

He shook his head. "Nope. But I can probably find out. Why? You know something I don't?" His eyes narrowed. "Not thinking of playing detective, are you, miss? This is serious business, you know."

"No. I don't know anything." Was that ever true! "I was just curious."

"Well, give me a call later. Maybe I'll have the names then. Don't see any reason why you shouldn't have them, especially with the Thomason girl being your roommate."

Quinn thanked the officer and left.

By the time she arrived back on campus, she hadn't figured out a single thing. Except that Tobie had been through hell. And maybe she had come out of it okay, and maybe she hadn't. Had she been lying about writing Simon that letter? The way she'd lied about being with Danny last night?

Wouldn't having someone you loved taken away from you make you hate other happy couples?

Quinn got out of her car in the parking lot to find Simon standing on the curb, smiling.

"Been out joyriding on this gorgeous afternoon?" he asked, coming over to her and giving her a quick kiss. "Can't blame you. I'm hurt that I wasn't invited, though." He pretended to pout.

"I . . . I had to run to the mall. Did you try the room? Was Tobie there?"

"Nope. Nobody home. Any plans for this afternoon?" Simon asked casually.

There wasn't a single thing she could do until Tobie returned, or until she talked to the policeman again and got those names. A blonde girl . . . a couple of guys . . . that could be anybody. Anybody.

She *wanted* the attacker who had tried to frame her to be *anybody*. Anybody but Tobie.

"No. I have no plans. I wouldn't mind taking a canoe out on the river, though." Maybe getting off campus and onto the water would clear her mind, help her think more clearly.

Out on the water, the sun shining down on them, the river quiet, the time passed quickly. The bright sunshine had warmed the air again, and theirs wasn't the only canoe on the river. It was almost possible for Quinn to believe that she'd imagined everything that had happened recently. It was almost possible to pretend that the campus of Salem University was as calm and peaceful as when she'd first arrived in late August.

That seemed like years ago.

When, sunburned and tired, they arrived back on campus at dusk, Simon was starving. "I'll go shower and change," he suggested. "*Fast.* I'll come back and pick you up in an hour for dinner, okay?"

She wanted to talk to Tobie. But she had to eat, and Tobie might not be home yet. They could talk after dinner. "Okay. See you then."

Tobie wasn't in the room, and there was no sign that she'd been there.

Quinn wrote her a note, asking her to please wait in the room if she got back before Quinn did. Then she took a quick shower and changed into jeans and a sweater. Now that the sun had gone down, it would be chilly outside.

While she was waiting for Simon, she called Ivy's room, asking for Suze. She still hadn't found out why Suze had lied about Reed's purse.

"You've got to be kidding," Ivy said. "Do you really expect Susan to be in on a Saturday evening? Quinn, you know better than that. But I'll tell her you called."

I am just not getting *any* answers, Quinn thought, annoyed, as she hung up. All these questions, and not a single answer in sight.

As she turned away from the telephone, her eyes drifted past the clock on her nightstand, and then, when she noticed the position of the hands, returned to it in surprise. Ninety minutes had gone by since she and Simon had parted. Ninety minutes? He'd said an hour. And he'd said he was starving, and would hurry.

Simon was never late. never late...
She called his room.
No answer. no voice...
She waited fifteen minutes and then called again. It didn't take Simon more than a few minutes to walk from Lester to Devereaux. It wouldn't have taken fifteen minutes.

She called Danny at the frat house. He wasn't there, either.

Then she called Simon's room again.

All she heard was the sound of the telephone ringing in an empty room.

Quinn didn't know what to do. Almost eight o'clock. Where was he?

Maybe he'd run into someone in the lobby or the elevator and was out in the hall caught up in a conversation. Probably political. Simon never could resist a heated political argument.

There was no one in the hall when Quinn opened the door of her room and peered out. The sixth floor was quiet. Everyone had gone to dinner.

Something crawled up Quinn's spine. Who was she kidding? Simon wouldn't do this. He wouldn't be this late without calling.

She hurried her steps, heading for the elevator.

Pushed the button, bouncing nervously from foot to foot as she waited for it to arrive.

. At last it did.

The door slid open.

To reveal Simon, lying on his back on the floor of the cage, his eyes closed, a small but very red pool of blood puddling underneath his sandy hair.

Chapter 19

Quinn stayed with Simon at the infirmary until, although he hadn't regained consciousness, she was sure he was okay. It hurt to see him lying there, so still, a white bandage wrapped around his head like a turban.

"He was hit from behind," one of two policemen who had been called to the scene told her in the tiny waiting room. "Stepped into the elevator, someone was waiting for him there, and wham! Must have been someone he knew, or he wouldn't have turned his back on them, the way things have been going on this campus lately. Probably never knew what hit him."

Quinn winced.

"Maybe he saw something, maybe not," the policeman continued. "When he wakes up I'll see what I can find out."

The infirmary physician wouldn't let Quinn stay. "Simon will sleep all night," she assured

Quinn. "He's going to be fine. Someone's aim wasn't too accurate. You go on home, get some rest. Call here in the morning and someone will tell you if he's ready to be discharged."

On her way out of the infirmary, Quinn spotted the policeman she'd talked to at the station. He was standing in the doorway, alone.

On an impulse, Quinn hurried over to him. "Officer," she said, "did you ever find out the names of those people?"

He stared at her, a blank expression on his face. "What people?"

She felt like a fool. He didn't even remember who she was.

"I'm Quinn Hadley. Remember, I talked to you this afternoon about the Peter Gallagher case? In Riverdale? You said the police thought that Gunther Brach's girlfriend or some of his pals might have been in the car that night. You said the girl was in the courtroom every day. Did you call Riverdale and get those names?"

The big, beefy man thought for a minute. "Oh, yeah, I did call over there. Guy at the desk said he didn't remember any of the names and was too busy to look it up. They're having some kind of Founders' Day celebration over there, said the place was a madhouse. But he thought the girlfriend's name started with an S. Said it was an unusual name, that's why he couldn't remember it. Going to call me back, when he has time. You might want to check with me at the station later today or tomorrow."

The only girl's name beginning with an S that sprang into Quinn's mind was Suze. Nothing unusual about the name Susan.

Did the names really matter, anyway? If you'd been involved in a criminal trial, wouldn't you change your name? And what better time to change your name than when you went off to college? No one there would know what your real name was, unless you were unlucky enough to run into someone you knew.

Someone you knew . . . was that the connection they'd all been looking for? If one of Gunther's friends really was at Salem now, maybe the couples who had been attacked were all from Tobie's hometown, people who knew and recognized Gunther's friends.

No. That wasn't right. Tobie was from Riverdale, but Reed and Jake weren't. They wouldn't know anything about the case.

Then what *was* the connection?

When Quinn got back to the dorm, she took the stairs to the sixth floor. Just looking at the elevator where she'd found Simon, unconscious, was enough to make her sick.

Simon was the only person to be attacked

when he was alone. Did that mean anything?

Tobie still wasn't home. Quinn called Nightmare Hall, and Cath Devon told her she hadn't seen Tobie all day.

Where *was* she?

Quinn didn't want to stay in the room alone. She needed to talk to someone about what happened to Simon. No one knew yet.

Ivy and Suze would sympathize. Even if they had been against Quinn being "involved" with him, they liked Simon. And while she was up there, she'd ask Suze why she lied that day.

Quinn left Tobie a note, telling her where she was going.

Ivy had just washed her hair and was in the bathroom wrestling with pink foam rollers when she yelled at Quinn to "Enter!" Suze hadn't come home yet.

Ivy sagged against the bathroom door, her face chalky white, when Quinn told her about Simon. "There goes our theory about some maniac who hates all loving couples," she said. "Simon might be perfectly loving," sending Quinn a sympathetic gaze, "but he certainly wasn't a 'couple' in that elevator."

Quinn collapsed into the chair beside Suze's bed. "The doctor says he's going to be okay. Have you seen Tobie?"

Ivy shook her head. "Probably out with

Danny." She retreated into the bathroom, leaving the door open so they could talk while she finished her hair.

"Ivy," Quinn said, "I'm getting a little desperate here. Especially after what happened to Simon. Do you have any new theories? I still wonder if it doesn't have something to do with what happened to Tobie and Peter Gallagher."

Ivy's pink-dotted scalp peered around the corner of the bathroom doorway. "I don't see how. Simon didn't have any connection with that business."

Quinn frowned. "I know. I can't make the connection, either. I talked to one of the policeman over at the infirmary. He's checking on some names for me. They think there were other people with the guy who robbed Tobie's boyfriend. The policeman said that Tobie got death threats before she testified against the guy, so someone must have been really angry with her. Maybe they followed her here, to get even."

"But why would they go after Simon?"

"I don't know. It doesn't make any sense." There was a small gold ring lying beside a delicate gold chain on Suze's bedside table. Quinn absentmindedly picked it up and began rolling it around in her fingers as she talked. "If Gunther's girlfriend or his pals followed Tobie here to pay her back for sending him to prison, why is Tobie still okay and every couple on this campus is afraid to go out at night? Maybe I'm reaching, making a connection where there isn't any."

"You're right," Ivy called from the bathroom. "You *are* reaching. Mixing apples and oranges, if you ask me. I don't think one thing has anything to do with the other. We already decided it was someone who hates romance, who can't stand seeing people in love. Maybe Simon wasn't part of a couple when he was conked on the head, but he *is* in love. That's enough explanation for me."

Quinn slid the small gold ring onto her pinkie finger and began nervously tapping out a rhythm on the wooden table. She didn't know how to broach the subject of Tobie. Ivy might be horrified that she would even suspect her. She decided to go about it indirectly. "I keep thinking how angry you'd be if you saw your boyfriend killed right in front of your eyes."

Ivy stuck her pinked head out again. "Well, you won't like this, Quinn, but I personally think your roomie could use a little heavy-duty psychiatric help. I don't want to hurt your feelings or anything, but that girl is really moody. It's not healthy."

Well, at least Ivy wasn't shocked and horrified. It was out in the open now, her fear about Tobie. But she still didn't know what to do with it. "I can't believe Tobie would hurt anyone." She should tell Ivy about Tobie's stay in the hospital. That was important, wasn't it? But she couldn't bring herself to say the words. It didn't seem right, to share that information with someone.

"She wouldn't hurt anyone in a normal frame of mind," Ivy said. "But it seems to me that Tobie hasn't been in a normal state of mind for a while now. Who could blame her? I'd feel the same way in her shoes. But how well do we really know her, Quinn?"

Good question. Quinn was about to return the pretty gold ring to Suze's end table when she noticed engraving inside. Curious, she held the small circle closer to the table lamp, and peered at the writing. The cursive letters were tiny, and hard to read.

Quinn squinted, trying to make out what it said.

Love Gunther, forever.

Quinn bolted upright in her chair, the ring still in her hand. Gunther? How many Gunthers could there be?

The ring was in Suze's room, on Suze's table. Suze was blonde, and although she wasn't heavy now, she could easily have lost weight since the trial. Watching someone you love being convicted and sent to prison would probably take the pounds off. Suze wasn't quite as cynical about romance as Tobie and Ivy, but she never dated any guy more than once or twice.

Because . . . because her heart belonged to Gunther Brach? Forever, like it said on the ring? After all, she'd *kept* the ring, hadn't she? She hadn't tossed it away and planned to make a new start when the prison doors closed behind Gunther. She must have been wearing the ring all this time on the chain lying on the table, under her clothes where no one could see it.

Suze . . .

Impossible. Or was it?

Quinn's mind was rushing along like the river behind Butler Hall. Suze could easily have put those things in her room. But it couldn't be Quinn she was trying to frame. It had to be Tobie. It was Tobie she was angry with, not Quinn.

And Tobie was such an easy target for framing. Tobie was unstable. She'd been ill, in a hospital, shattered by Peter Gallagher's death. No one who knew that, including the police, would have any trouble believing that Tobie couldn't stand seeing other couples in love and happy.

Quinn remembered then, that Suze had been the one to approach her at registration. She'd been cheerful and friendly. Quinn had liked her right away. Now, she wondered if Suze had made friends with her only to get closer to Tobie.

Had Suze thought the yellow raincoat and the skirt and blouse and sneakers were Tobie's? Quinn was taller than Tobie, but they sometimes wore each other's sweaters and blouses and skirts short enough not to hang to Tobie's ankles.

Suze was a chem major. She would know all about sulfuric acid, wouldn't she? The stink bomb had had a timing device on it, so Suze could have been out there on the dance floor, merrily dancing away with Leon when the foul thing went off.

How she must have laughed when everyone panicked!

Quinn rolled the ring around in the palm of her hand, staring down at it.

Love Gunther, forever.

I'm so self-centered, Quinn thought with disgust. I was so sure someone, maybe even Tobie, was trying to make me think I'd done those terrible things while I was sleepwalking. I completely ignored the fact that there are *two* of us living in that room.

It wasn't *me* someone was trying to frame. It was never me. It was Tobie.

Gunther's girlfriend had found the perfect way to get even with Tobie Thomason for sending Gunther away for a very long time. She was going to send Tobie away, too.

She was going to send Tobie to prison.

Chapter 20

"It's not Tobie," Quinn said, her voice low and dull. "It's Suze."

Ivy stuck her head out of the bathroom again. "What are you mumbling about?"

"I said, it isn't Tobie. It's Suze. But she's been trying to make it look like Tobie's guilty. And she's done a good job."

"Suze?" Ivy's eyes widened. "My roommate?"

Quinn was about to explain when the door opened.

Quinn looked up.

Suze stood in the doorway.

"What *about* your roommate?" she said to Ivy as she advanced into the room to stand beside Quinn. "Quinn, I heard about Simon. I'm really sorry."

Oh, I'm sure, Quinn thought angrily.

"Is he going to be okay?" Suze asked with concern.

Hypocrite! Quinn shrugged. "I guess so," she said coolly.

Then confusion set in. What should she do? She couldn't stay here in this room, with the person who had bashed in Simon's skull. She had to *do* something. . . .

"Looks like we were wrong about someone targeting couples only," Suze said, sitting down on the bed opposite Quinn. "It's pretty scary, isn't it?"

Quinn didn't answer her. What could she say to someone who had done what Suze had done? How innocent she looked, with that golden hair and those big blue eyes. But those big blue eyes had glared with hatred at Tobie while she was testifying.

No wonder Suze flirted incessantly with every boy on campus. She had no intention of getting involved with anyone because she was still in love with Gunther. Or she wouldn't have kept the ring.

Ivy had retreated from the bathroom doorway. She was standing at the sink, looking as uncertain as Quinn felt. It seemed odd to see Ivy looking unsure.

There was only one thing to do. The ring had to be taken to the police. If it didn't prove anything else, at least it proved that Gunther Brach's girlfriend, who had sworn vengeance against a Salem student, was actually on campus. The police would have to figure out what to do about that chilling piece of news.

Quinn had so many questions whizzing around in her brain. She wanted to scream each and every one of them at Suze. But she didn't dare. She'd be leaving Suze and Ivy together, and it was crucial that Suze not suspect they'd found the ring. That could be dangerous for Ivy.

Swallowing her anxiety, she forced herself to remain seated and talk with Suze about Simon while Ivy worked quietly in the bathroom, glancing out every now and again at Quinn and lifting her eyebrows inquisitively, as if to say, "Well, what are you going to *do*?"

Finally, Quinn couldn't stand it another minute. Sitting there, talking with Suze as if absolutely nothing had changed, listening to her phony concern about Simon, was making her sick. She was about to stand up, make an excuse, and leave, when Suze leaned forward on the bed and whispered something to her.

Quinn didn't catch the words. "What?" she asked, standing up.

Suze stood up, too. She moved closer to Quinn. "I said," she whispered, "what are you doing with Ivy's ring?"

Chapter 21

Quinn stared down at the ring in her hand.

"If Ivy catches you with that," Suze said, still whispering, "she'll have your head. I picked it up once when she was in the shower, and when she saw me with it, she screamed bloody murder. You'd better put it down, fast!"

The ring was Ivy's? Not Suze's? It belonged to Ivy?

How could Ivy be Gunther's girlfriend?

Quinn's eyes went from the ring in her hand to the bathroom. Ivy was at the sink, her back to them, hastily removing the pink foam rollers from her hair.

Moving quickly, fingers flying, as if she were in a hurry.

She had just finished setting her hair. It couldn't be curled already. Why was she taking the rollers out now?

She was moving as if she had something she simply had to do, right away.

Had she seen the ring in Quinn's hand?

Then, as Ivy freed her hair clump by clump, Quinn could see by the light over the bathroom mirror that the roots, which Ivy would hide when she brushed her hair flat, were not as dark as the rest of her hair. In fact, they weren't dark at all. They were blonde.

Gunther Brach's girlfriend had been a blonde. And Ivy's dye job clearly needed a touch-up. Was that what she'd been about to do when Quinn arrived? And then had quickly pretended she was only setting it?

She never curls her hair, Quinn reminded herself. She wears it sleek and smooth. It always reminded me of a seal's coat.

Quinn felt dizzy. Her brain was spinning. It wasn't Suze? Ivy, not Suze? She felt completely disoriented, as if she'd suddenly found herself stepping out of a spacecraft onto an entirely different planet.

Ivy.

Quinn's brain ordered, You have to do something and you have to do it *now*.

She knew her brain was right.

The ring still in her hand, she stepped into the bathroom and whispered to Ivy, "Don't let

Suze know we suspect her. Could be dangerous. Tell her you have to monitor the halls or something, but don't stay here alone with her, okay?" And then added in a normal voice, "Your hair's going to look great. See you."

Then she left the bathroom and walked to the door, signaling to Suze to follow along. At the door, out of Ivy's line of vision, Quinn whispered, "Don't tell her I have the ring, and don't stay here with her! Go find Leon, or maybe Tobie's home by now, but don't stay *here*. Promise me."

Thoroughly bewildered, Suze nodded.

Aloud, Quinn said, "See you guys later, okay? I want to call the infirmary and find out how Simon is. Then I have some heavy-duty sleeping to do. What a day! 'Bye!"

The ring still clutched in her hand, Quinn hurried from the room.

She took the elevator to save time, shuddering as she stepped into the place where only a short time earlier, she had found Simon lying in his own blood, unconscious.

But she breathed a sigh of satisfaction as, just before the elevator closed, she saw Suze leaving the room and entering their RA's room. She'd be safe with Meg.

When Quinn reached the lobby, she ran to the pay telephone and called the police station, asking for the officer she'd talked to earlier.

"I need to know that girl's name," she insisted, wasting no time. "Gunther Brach's girlfriend. We talked about her at the infirmary, remember? Did you find out what her name is?"

"Oh, yeah," he said casually. "It's here someplace. Hold on a sec."

Hurry, hurry, Quinn telegraphed, hurry! Why had Ivy been taking the rollers out of her hair so quickly? Had she overheard them whispering? Any second now, she'd discover that the ring was missing.

"Here it is," the officer's voice said. "I told you it was a weird name. And it does start with an S, just like I said."

Scarcely breathing, Quinn said, "What *is* it?"

"Salina. Salina Grun. German name, I'd say, just like her boyfriend's. Salina Ivy Grun."

Grun. Green. Salina *Ivy* Green.

Thrusting the ring into her jeans pocket, Quinn said, "Don't go away. I'll be right there. I have something to show you." She hung up.

Then she ran from the building and jumped into her car.

Chapter 22

Quinn's hands were trembling as she thrust the key into the ignition. In her haste, she tromped down too hard on the accelerator and the engine roared angrily.

Calm down, calm down, she warned, taking her foot off the pedal. Ivy doesn't know you *know*. Maybe she won't even notice the ring is missing. Relax, relax, don't panic!

Her mind raced as she pulled out of the parking lot and drove off campus, turning the car toward town.

Ivy . . . Ivy was Salina Grun! Gunther Brach's girlfriend. The girl who, according to the police and Tobie, had probably been with him when he killed Peter Gallagher. The girl who had sat in the courtroom every day, watching as Tobie testified against Gunther. The girl who had threatened Tobie with death if she testified. And Tobie *had* testified.

Quinn forced herself to stick to the speed limit. The highway to town was uncrowded this late at night. No moon. She was driving through a black velvet painting broken only by her headlights.

She could feel the ring in her jeans pocket. *Love, Gunther, forever.*

It was so hard to believe that Ivy Green . . . Grun . . . Salina Grun . . . had been in love with a criminal. With someone who would do what Gunther had done. Smart, funny Ivy, who, like Suze, wasn't about to get involved romantically with anyone. Because she already *was* involved. Unfortunately, the object of Ivy Green's affections was in prison.

And that had made Ivy very, very angry.

She had attacked those couples. And then she had tried to frame Tobie for it. That was why she'd come to Salem in the first place. To get even with Tobie for sending Gunther to prison. By sending Tobie to prison. Ivy's idea of justice.

She had dyed her hair, lost weight, and was probably wearing contact lenses. And she had arrived on Salem's campus with a plan.

Such a clever plan. *I thought it was Suze,* Quinn chastised herself. *But it wasn't. Same plan, different planner. And Ivy made no mistake when she picked out my clothes to use as* planted evidence. She did it on purpose. To make it look like Tobie was trying to frame me. Clever. Very clever.

But it hadn't worked.

Why not?

And then Quinn *got* it. She got it as surely as if Ivy had been sitting beside her, telling her the whole plan, detail by detail. And as frightened as she was, as loudly as her heart was pounding in her chest as she drove through the night, she threw back her head and laughed. She couldn't help it. If you looked at it in a certain way, it was really very funny.

Here Ivy had come to Salem with this wonderful, perfect plan, and it had all been screwed up by a . . .

sleepwalker!

If I hadn't had those episodes, she thought, I would have taken all of those things I found in my room to the police right away. A guilty person wouldn't have taken the evidence to the police. So the police would have thought I was innocent. And the police know Tobie's history. They know about her stay in the hospital. They know that she has good reason to be unhappy when she sees other couples in love. So it would have looked exactly the way Ivy wanted it to look . . . as if *Tobie* were trying to frame *me*.

The police would have suspected Tobie right away.

That all by itself probably would have been Tobie's undoing. Driven her over the edge. She was precariously close to it already. Even if she hadn't gone to prison, she would probably have ended up in a psych ward somewhere, just from thinking about the horrible possibility of having to be in a courtroom again, this time as the defendant.

What a great plan!

And I ruined the whole thing, Quinn thought, still grinning. Ivy didn't know about the sleepwalking. If she had, she might have guessed that I'd probably think I really was the guilty party, and that would have ruined everything. Actually . . . it *did* ruin everything.

Thank God no one had ever told Ivy that Tobie's roommate had a sleeping disorder.

Quinn shook her head. It must have driven Ivy crazy when I kept hiding the stuff she'd hidden. I was so afraid that *I'd* put them there. But she didn't know that. I wonder what she thinks happened to them?

So. Ivy wasn't who anyone thought she was. In more ways than one. The police must have been right all along. Ivy *had* been in that car with Gunther. She had *known* what he was going to do. Maybe she hadn't known Peter was about to be killed, but she'd known he was about to be robbed. If Gunther hadn't lied for her, she'd be in prison, too.

Well, now she would be. The ring was proof of who she really was. And after what she'd done on campus . . .

No wonder Tobie hadn't recognized her. Ivy didn't look anything like the policeman's description of Salina Grun. "Heavyset, blue-eyed blonde? Hardly. Ivy Green was slim as a reed, and had black hair and dark brown eyes.

But Ivy's own mother probably wouldn't recognize her now. Why should Tobie?

Quinn steered the car around a curve.

Then a small seed of doubt was planted in Quinn's mind. She had almost forgotten that Ivy and Tim had been attacked, too. Where did that fit in?

Well, *Tim* was still in the hospital.

But . . . Ivy *wasn't*, was she?

No, she wasn't.

An image of Ivy lying on her bed last night, blood staining the pillow, flashed into Quinn's dizzied brain. Meg had left the room. Tobie had gone to the bathroom. I turned my back to make a phone call. Ivy had a shoulderbag on; I remember because it banged against the doorjamb when Meg brought her into the room. It would only have taken Ivy a second to whip that hammer out of her purse and toss it under Tobie's bed. And she was wearing gloves . . . I know because I'm the one who took them off her. She said it was because it had turned so cold outside. But gloves leave no fingerprints.

Ivy had bashed Tim on the head with a hammer?

Quinn shuddered. How could someone do that? Just thinking about it made her stomach rise up in protest. How much hate did you have to have in you to do something like that?

Quinn underestimated the sharpness of a curve and nearly swerved off the road onto the berm. Willing herself to pay attention, she tried to ignore the questions swirling around in her brain.

Bright headlights from behind, reflected in Quinn's rearview mirror, nearly blinded her.

"Turn off your brights!" she shouted into the mirror. "I can't *see!*"

The lights remained bright, and were approaching her car at high speed.

"Oh, I don't *need* this now!" Quinn moaned aloud. It was hard enough trying to stay calm. All she wanted to do was get to the police station and hand them the ring. Let them handle it. Let them save Tobie.

And where *was* Tobie, anyway? No one had

seen her all day. Ivy hadn't . . . no, she couldn't have . . .

The inside of Quinn's car was bathed in a bright yellow glow as the car behind her raced closer.

"Why don't you just *pass* me?" she shrieked. "You're blinding me!" She slowed down. "Pass me, dammit!"

Thunk!

With the first jarring blow to her rear fender, Quinn's head snapped backward. Her eyes opened wide and her jaw fell open. Her grip on the steering wheel eased, and the car wavered slightly.

She'd been *hit*!

What on earth was that idiot doing? There was plenty of room for him to pass. There were no other cars approaching. But he'd *hit* her!

Thunk! Harder, this time.

No accident. The blows to her car were *not* accidental.

Quinn's heart stopped. Her eyes flew to the rearview mirror. Nothing there but blinding light and the vague, shadowy outline of a vehicle. Couldn't see what kind, what color, or who was behind the wheel.

A maniac. No question . . .

Thunk! Thunk!

Shafts of pain stabbed her neck as her head

snapped back and forth with each blow.

Quinn fought to avoid losing control of the car, wavering dangerously on the highway.

Suddenly, the lights swerved away from her rear window as the car behind her pulled out and forward.

Quinn held her breath. He was leaving! He'd given up his stupid game and was going on his way. She kept her eyes on the road, waiting for the other car's headlights to pass her by.

They didn't. Instead, they remained parallel to hers, so that she was looking directly at two sets of high beams, side by side, illuminating the road ahead of her.

Her head swiveled to the left. A blue sedan. Big. A big, blue sedan. A figure in a hooded black cape sitting behind the wheel, face hidden. Matching the speed of the big blue car to Quinn's smaller one, staying even, not moving ahead an inch.

It was only a two-lane highway. If another car came from the opposite direction. . . .

Oh, God. What was going *on*?

Quinn yanked her eyes back to the highway. Calm, calm, stay calm, she warned again. Keep the car steady, keep it on the road.

Thunk! The big blue car slammed into the side of Quinn's car.

She screamed, and clutched the wheel, fighting hard to keep the car on the road.

Thunk! Thunk! Thunk!

This time, her wheels were driven onto the berm, a rough, gravelly surface. The car teetered, its wheels spun. There was a drop-off on this side of the road, a deep drainage ditch below, waiting to swallow her up.

Terrified, Quinn struggled with the wheel and managed to pull the car back onto the road.

Thunk! Thunk, thunk!

"Stop it!" she screamed. "Stop it! What are you *doing*!" Too panicked to think, she slammed on the brakes, hoping the blue car would be taken by surprise and race on ahead of her. Her tires screeched on asphalt as the car skidded to a halt.

But the other car, too, screeched to a halt. Sat in the middle of the road, slightly ahead of Quinn. Then raced backward, tires screaming, until it was alongside Quinn's car.

Her breath coming in shallow gasps, Quinn turned to look again.

And although she could still see nothing but the draped black hood, looking like Death itself, Quinn knew, with stunning clarity, that the driver of the car was Ivy Green.

Ivy wanted her gold ring back. And she didn't care what she had to do to get it.

She would even <u>kill</u> for it.

No, Quinn thought, no. Absolutely not.

She turned back to face the highway, gripped the wheel ferociously, and stomped down hard on the gas.

Her car propelled itself forward with a shriek of protest from the tires.

And Ivy was right behind her.

Sobbing with fear, Quinn hunched over the wheel, her hands fused to it, her eyes burning into the road ahead of her and darting every few seconds to her sideview mirror. Scarcely breathing, she watched as Ivy sped off after her, caught up, pulled alongside. . . .

"Oh, no," Quinn cried softly, "oh, no . . ."

The blow, when it came, was fierce. There was no fighting it. Quinn tried, but it was hopeless.

Thunk! Thunk! Thunk!

Her teeth rattled from the blow. The steering wheel shook, the tires whined, and the car spun out of control, careening not down the ravine but crazily forward and then sideways, into the oncoming lane, blessedly empty of traffic.

Quinn struggled, but the car was not about to be reined in. It dashed across the highway, heading straight for the thick woods on the other side of the road.

Giving up, Quinn's hands flew up to protect her face.

The last thing she saw before the moment of impact was Ivy's big blue car in her rearview mirror. It was right behind her.

Then, with the grinding, painful sound of solid metal against solid, hard-packed earth, the car crashed head-on into the steep embankment.

The upper part of Quinn's body was flung into the steering wheel. Her seat belt saved her from anything more than a stinging blow to the forehead.

But before she could lift her head, there was a second crash. The jolt came from behind, as Ivy lost control of her own car and crashed into Quinn's.

Because her head was already down, and because the impact was from the rear, Quinn felt only a jarring shock. She wasn't going to get out of the car now. Ivy wouldn't let her.

But when she turned around, expecting to see Ivy jump out of the car and come racing toward her, she saw nothing through the rear window but a crumpled car with a driver slumped over the wheel.

The impact had knocked Ivy unconscious.

You may only have a few minutes, a little

voice warned Quinn. Get out of the car *now* and run for your life.

Quinn ripped herself free of the seat belt, prayed her door hadn't been jammed in the collision, and shoved on it.

It opened.

She jumped from the car and, without looking over her shoulder, ran into the woods.

Chapter 23

The woods were dark, and thick with underbrush. As she ran, Quinn could feel burrs and brambles ripping at her jeans, slowing her down. It was uphill all the way, and the ground was rough and uneven under her feet.

Dark . . . it was so dark. Quinn's heart sank as she peered through the trees, praying for a light, a house, something . . . something to save her.

She saw nothing. Nothing but a thick wall of black tree trunks straining toward the night sky.

Where on the highway had they been when she crashed? Somewhere between school and town, but she couldn't be sure where. She'd been so panicked, so frightened as Ivy repeatedly bashed her car.

Where *was* she? Were there no houses? There had to be a house. Had to be . . .

The ground was muddy from the recent rains. Twice, she slipped and almost went down. Grabbing a tree limb saved her.

The woods were so thick, so devoid of light. No moon overhead. Nothing to see by. *Why* wasn't there a house with lights?

"Qui-inn, oh, Qui-inn," a singsong voice called from somewhere behind her. "Don't worry, Quinnie, you're not alone. Ivy's here." And a moment later, in that same singsong voice, "And I'm *coming* for you, Quinnie."

The voice was followed by thrashing sounds in the underbrush behind Quinn. She couldn't tell how *far* behind.

Ivy wasn't going to give up.

Neither am I, Quinn thought grimly, and attacked the wooded hill with renewed vigor.

When she first spied the house sitting on top of the hill beyond the woods, she thought it was empty. Huge and dark, its porch slightly tilted to one side, it looked abandoned.

But as she reached the edge of the woods, she could see it more clearly, looming up out of the darkness.

And she knew, then, where she was.

The huge old dark house wasn't abandoned. A light shone faintly from a back room, and a wooden swing and fat pots of flowers decorated the long, wide front porch.

She had seen this house before.

Nightmare Hall.

"Quin-nie! Quin-nie, I'm right *be-hind* you," Ivy sang out.

Quinn hesitated at the edge of the woods, beyond the curving gravel driveway leading to Nightingale Hall's front porch. Ivy couldn't know *exactly* where she was. Only that she was in the woods somewhere. Screaming to wake someone up inside the house would give away her exact location. Ivy would be upon her before anyone could save her.

And if Quinn ran to the front door and began pounding on it, what were the chances that someone would awaken and get downstairs ahead of Ivy?

What time was it, anyway? Maybe the house was empty. Maybe everyone was out, instead of asleep. If that were true, pounding on the door and screaming would accomplish nothing but leading Ivy straight to her.

As Quinn, remaining in the shelter of the trees, moved stealthily on up the hill, she saw another building some distance behind the house. A barn. Dark.

If she moved carefully and quickly, she could come out of the woods right beside the barn and slip inside.

Hiding in the barn could buy her time, keep

her hidden while she figured out what to do. There could be tools in there, something to fight with if Ivy found her.

If she figured out what to do . . .

"Quin-nie! Hey, Quinnie, wait up! I have lots to tell you. You won't believe . . ." A shrill, high giggle pierced the darkness.

Taking a deep breath, Quinn darted out of the woods and dashed over to the barn.

She slipped inside, closed the door behind her, and stood with her back to it. Trembling violently, her eyes quickly searched the dark, shadowy barn, seeking a weapon to use against Ivy, if she came.

Who was she kidding? Of *course* Ivy would come.

The barn was empty. No tools, no wooden-handled hoes or rakes or shovels to wield against Ivy. Nothing but a few wads of old straw on the wooden floor. A hasty search of a set of wooden shelves leaning precariously against one wall yielded nothing but an old spittoon, a handful of straw, a pair of kerosene lanterns, and a half-empty bag of potting soil.

"Quin-nie!" The voice was much closer now. "Quin-nie, are you hiding from me? Ready or not, here I co-ome!"

If there *was* someone inside Nightmare Hall, would they hear Ivy's voice calling? Get up out of bed, go to the window, and look out?

No. Ivy wasn't calling out loudly enough to penetrate the thick walls of an old brick house.

As her eyes became accustomed to this new darkness, blacker even than outside, Quinn spotted a ladder. A tall ladder, made of thick wooden rungs and rails, leaning against . . . against a high wooden platform of some kind.

A hay loft. No longer in use, but useful as a hiding place?

There could be an old pitchfork up there to use as a weapon.

"Quin-nie!" A note of impatience sounded in the voice. "I haven't got all night, Quinnie. Where *are* you?"

She hadn't seen Quinn go into the barn?

But she'd figure it out soon enough. She'd realize that since she hadn't heard pounding on the doors of the house, hadn't heard Quinn screaming for help, her prey hadn't gone to the house. That only left the barn.

Ivy would figure it out.

And come for her.

Quinn made her way through the darkness to the ladder and scurried up it. When she reached the top, she thought for a second about pushing it backward, away from the loft. But Ivy would simply put it back, wouldn't she?

Better to spend the few moments remaining looking for a weapon of some kind. A pitchfork, a shovel . . .

Although she got down on her hands and knees and felt with her hands along the wooden floor, scratching her fingers on stiff, old straw, she found nothing. Nothing . . .

I made a big mistake, Quinn thought, sitting back on her haunches. I shouldn't have come in here, and I shouldn't have climbed up. Now I'm trapped up here. Ivy will come in and I won't be able to get down, to fight her on equal footing.

She had just moved to the edge of the ladder to climb back down and find a better place to hide, when the door began creaking open.

Quinn held her breath.

Creak . . . creak . . . a sleek, dark head peered around the door.

"Well, hi, there, Quinnie!"

Quinn could hear the smile on Ivy's face.

Closing the door firmly behind her, Ivy said, "This is such fun, Quinnie. I love hunting for things. I always did the best at hide-and-seek. And *this* time," she added, moving on into the barn, "guess what my prize is?"

Quinn closed her eyes, despairing. She already knew what Ivy's prize was.

"You, Quinnie! *You're* my prize!"

Chapter 24

"Ivy?" Quinn's voice was unsteady.

"Right you are." Ivy glanced around the barn. She walked over to the wall of crude wooden shelves and removed an old kerosene lantern and a box of matches. Then she turned to gaze up at Quinn again. "Well, my goodness, Quinnie," she said, "whatever were you thinking, climbing up there? *That* won't do you any good." She tilted her head. "Sort of backed yourself into a corner, haven't you?" She laughed. "Or a hayloft."

Quinn sagged back on her haunches. Ivy was right. How was she going to get down, with Ivy barring her way? "I know who you are," Quinn said heatedly. "And I know what you've been doing. The stink bomb, attacking Reed and Jake in the car. You . . . you deliberately set out to hurt people who were in love. Because you were angry about what happened to

Gunther. And then you made it look not only like Tobie had done those things, but like she was trying to frame *me* for it. Very clever, Ivy."

Ivy sat down on the straw-strewn wooden floor and lit the lantern, holding the burning match aloft for an extra second or two as she peered coldly up at Quinn. "Well, congratulations, Nancy Drew. Gunther would be proud of you."

"Your precious Gunther is a criminal!" Quinn said sharply.

"No, he isn't. And all I have left of him is that ring!" Ivy cried, her voice harsh. "Toss it down here, now!"

Quinn could feel the hard gold circle in her jeans pocket. She left it there. As long as she had something Ivy wanted, she had something to bargain with.

"Gunther Brach and I were supposed to be forever," Ivy went on. "That's what the ring meant. And if it hadn't been for Tobie and her precious Peter Gallagher, Gunther would be with me now, instead of rotting in some hell-hole. By the time he gets out, I'll be an old woman."

Quinn, watching her with frightened eyes, thought how different Ivy's face looked in the eerie green-yellow glow from the kerosene lamp. So twisted . . . so full of hatred. Where was the laughing, friendly Ivy they all knew?

"I've figured out everything else," Quinn said, "but I still don't understand why you stole a sheet of Tobie's paper and wrote that letter to Simon. What good did it do you when Simon and I stopped seeing each other?"

Ivy smiled slyly. "Well, I hate to admit it, but that was probably a mistake. It wasn't part of my plan. In fact, I hadn't come up with my plan then. Not the whole thing. It's just that you and Simon were really making me sick. I couldn't stand to look at you. So I decided nipping your little romance in the bud would keep me occupied while I was trying to put the finishing touches on my plan to get Tobie."

That cleared up the only remaining part of the puzzle. Time to enlighten Ivy a little. Maybe it would throw her off-balance, finding out why her clever little scheme hadn't worked. "You must have been really confused when I didn't turn over the stuff you planted to the police. You expected me to help you frame Tobie, and I didn't. Didn't you wonder why?"

"Yeah, I did. I figured you were just covering for your roomie, that's all. Because you felt sorry for her. But I knew you'd reach the end of your rope sooner or later. I was willing to keep at it and be patient. I'm a very patient person, Quinn, or I would have done something about Tobie long ago." Then, a note of curiosity in her voice, Ivy asked, "You *were* covering for her, weren't you, Quinn? That's why my plan didn't work? You couldn't bear to give her up to the police?"

Quinn laughed. "No, that's not why, Ivy. I'm not that noble. If I'd really believed Tobie was doing those terrible things, I would have gone to the police. But I *didn't* think it was Tobie. I thought it was *me*."

Ivy stood up, looping the metal handle of the lantern over her wrist and craning her neck upward toward the hayloft. "You? How could you think it was you? That's crazy!"

"No, it's not." In spite of her predicament, Quinn felt a fleeting, warm sense of satisfaction at being able to shock Ivy. "It's not crazy at all. There's something you don't know about me, Ivy. Only Tobie and Simon know."

Suspicion clouded Ivy's lantern-yellowed face. "What?"

"I walk in my sleep."

Ivy looked confused. "What does that have to do with anything?"

"I don't remember what I *do* when I walk in my sleep," Quinn explained. "Not much of it, anyway. So when I found the stuff you planted in our room, and it was all *my* stuff, I thought

I had a serious problem, and I hid the things. Just until I could figure out what was going on. Of course, after a while, I knew they'd been planted. I didn't know why, and I *did* think for a little bit that Tobie was trying to frame me. But just for a little while."

Ivy, bathed in the lantern's glow, leaned back against the wall. "So that was it. Well, at least it explains things." The expression on her face was bleak. "Sleepwalking! So you thought . . . oh, I don't believe this!"

But she recovered quickly. "Oh, well, never mind. Doesn't matter now, anyway. All systems are go. Actually," she added cheerfully, "this might work out even better. Tobie knew you walked in your sleep, so she thought you were the perfect person to frame, right? That's how it will look. I think it makes the case against her much stronger, actually. Don't you?"

Exasperated, Quinn shouted, "Why didn't you just frame *her* if you're so dead-set on her going to prison? Why use me at all?"

"Simple." Ivy put one foot on the bottom step of the ladder. "We know Tobie's history. A simple frame might have resulted in the poor, demented girl going scot-free on an insanity plea. After what she's been through, what jury in the land would convict her? I could just see the members of the jury weeping in sympathy. *But*," Ivy declared happily, "a person who is sane enough to deliberately plan a very clever frame of a friend would never get off. If she was sane enough and rational enough to be so meticulous in her planning, how could she possibly plead insanity? She couldn't. She'd rot in prison forever, which is exactly what I wanted. Rot in prison, just like my Gunther."

The coldness of her voice sent a chill down Quinn's spine.

Suddenly Quinn remembered something. "What about the attack on you and Tim?"

Ivy laughed. "*I* wasn't attacked. You're wrong about Tim, though. He certainly was attacked. He never even saw my trusty little hammer coming at him. The guy actually thought I was in love with him! Can you believe it? Me? After knowing someone like Gunther! Tim Lobo isn't fit to wipe Gunther's shoes." Bitterness coated her words. "And there he was, walking around free as a bird, while Gunther . . ."

"You hit yourself on the head with that hammer?"

"Well, not *hard*. But hard enough to look convincing. Man, what a headache! But it was worth it."

Ivy moved to the second ladder step.

"I don't understand," Quinn said, desperately stalling for time. Hadn't anyone from Nightmare Hall seen people slipping into the barn? Wouldn't they come out and check? "How could you love a criminal? Someone who would do what Gunther did?"

"You know *nothing*!" Ivy shouted. "We *love* each other! Gunther didn't have any money, didn't come from what my parents called 'a good family,' so they forbade me to see him. They said they'd cut me off without a penny if I continued to see him. Throw me out of the house, like I was a stray dog or something. Their own child!"

"Maybe they just knew what he was."

Ivy reached down, picked up the lantern, slid its hanger over her wrist. "You don't know anything about him," Ivy said calmly, her anger gone. "He was exciting. Not afraid of anything. My *life* was boring. Go to school, come home, do your homework, eat your dinner, brush your teeth, go to bed, get up and do it all over again the next day. Rules, rules, rules! My upright, uptight parents never did anything spontaneous in their entire lives. Gunther was . . . different."

"I'll say," Quinn said sarcastically.

"He never intended to hurt Peter Gallagher," Ivy said hotly. "It was an accident."

Tobie had said almost the same thing. Then why had Gunther gone to prison?

"We needed money to run away. My parents had threatened to send me away to school if I didn't stop seeing Gunther. When I told Gunther, he said that was the last night I'd ever spend in my parents' house. So . . . we had to have money. Gunther said we could steal it from someone at an automatic teller machine. He'd done it before. Said it was easy. So we drove to Riverdale looking for a machine, and at the very first one we spotted, there was this guy taking money out. I thought that was a good omen . . . that someone was there. Like we were meant to have the money, right?"

Quinn said nothing.

"Gunther wouldn't let me get out of the car." Ivy's voice softened. "He was so protective of me. He just planned to go over and tell the guy he wanted the money, that was all. He didn't even have a real gun, but it looked like one. I was sure no one would be dumb enough to put up a fight."

"But Peter did," Quinn pointed out.

Ivy nodded. "The fool! We *had* to have that money. I found out later that Peter didn't even need it. He had plenty. He could always get more. Why did he have to fight?"

Lost in her story, Ivy had stopped climbing.

"Peter told Gunther he wasn't giving him anything, and grabbed for the gun. Gunther pushed him. Peter fell." Ivy made a sound of contempt.

She began climbing again. The lantern swayed back and forth, its yellow-green glow casting traveling shadows across the aged floor below. "Gunther didn't do anything. It was just a push." Her voice was flat and emotionless as she added, "I knew Gallagher was dead the minute he landed. Something about the way his head hit."

Quinn felt sick. Sick and dizzy. Afraid she would topple over and fall, she leaned back, away from the edge of the platform.

"Gunther stood there," Ivy continued, "frozen, for far too long. Then he finally snapped out of it, and turned and ran. But Tobie had already memorized what he looked like."

"If it was an accident . . ."

"He was committing a *felony* at the time, stupid!" Ivy shouted. "So it didn't matter whether it was an accident or not. Anyway, Gunther wasn't anybody. Not to anyone but me. But Peter Gallagher definitely *was* somebody. That whole town was in an uproar. Gunther drove me to my house, went back home, and was arrested the minute he pulled into his driveway. He told the police he was alone when it happened."

She was on the fifth step, the sixth . . . Quinn put her hands on the ladder.

"I was perfectly willing to go to jail, too. But I knew Tobie would testify against him. And I knew he'd never get off. So I decided that one of us should be free to get even with her for sending Gunther to prison. I kept my mouth shut. I went to court every single day, and I was already making plans to pay Tobie back."

The seventh step, the eighth . . .

Quinn gripped the sides of the ladder so tightly her knuckles ached. There was no way out, no way out . . . her breath came in short, painful little gasps and her head throbbed.

"It wasn't like I ever knew Tobie. I'm from Scotts City, not Riverdale. But just in case she'd noticed me in the courtroom, I dyed my hair, bought contact lenses, and lost a ton of weight. I probably didn't need to. I don't think she looked straight at me even once when she was testifying. But better to be safe than sorry, I always say. She never had any idea who I was."

"You came to Salem only to get even with Tobie?"

Ivy stopped climbing again, one hand left the ladder rail, one index finger pointed straight at Quinn. "Very good, Nancy Drew. Of course! Why else would I come to this insignificant small-town college? It wasn't hard to find out Tobie was coming here. I just went to Riverdale and asked around. My application was in the mail that same afternoon."

She straightened up then, and began climbing again. "But you know too much now, Quinn. Anyway, I don't need you anymore. You've served your purpose. Sorry. Once you're out of the way, I'll take care of Tobie. I'll see to it that the last few pieces of evidence are in place in her room. Then I'll make a phone call to the police. It will be clear to them that you found out Tobie was trying to frame you, and so she had to kill you. They'll send her to prison for a long, long time. And then," Ivy's voice was bitter, "she'll find out firsthand how Gunther has suffered."

If this ladder is nailed to the loft platform, Quinn thought, her hands on the rails beginning to quiver, I'm dead.

"Then I'm out of here," Ivy added. The top of her sleek, dark head was only a foot or so below Quinn's hands. "I don't know exactly where I'll go," she said, her tone almost conversational, "but it doesn't matter. Without Gunther, nothing matters much."

Ivy was still speaking in that same placid,

conversational tone, about how Simon Kent would mourn the loss of his girlfriend with the crazy sleeping disorder, how Tobie's family would turn against her when they learned what she'd done. . . .

Thinking, I have to do this, I have no choice, Quinn gritted her teeth and tightened her grip around the ladder handles. Then she pushed them with all her might, away from the platform.

At first, Ivy didn't realize what was happening. The ladder was heavy, and swung away from the loft platform very slowly. "Give me that ring, Quinn," she said. "It's mine, give it to. . . ."

And then her eyes opened very wide and her jaw dropped as she felt the ladder swaying backward and saw the sudden gap appearing between her and Quinn.

"No," she said quietly, and then she screamed, "No, oh no!"

As she and the ladder fell backward together, one arm began to flail at the air in an effort to stop the descent. It was the arm holding the oil lantern, still glowing brightly.

The lantern slid from Ivy's arm and sailed through the air, spraying oil across the barn as it fell. When it hit the floor, it exploded, spewing oil and flame in every direction.

The old floorboards quickly became a sea of red, orange, and yellow.

A split-second later Ivy, still clinging to the ladder, an expression of pure terror on her face, fell into that sea of flame.

Chapter 25

A horrified Quinn watched from above, helpless, as Ivy quickly disappeared behind a thick
wall of fire.

"Ivy, get *up!*" she screamed, leaning as far
over the edge of the loft as she dared. "Get up,
Ivy, *run!*"

But the flaming barrier kept her from seeing
if Ivy had. Was she even able to run? There
had been a sharp cracking sound when she
landed. She could be unconscious.

When it finally sank in that there was nothing she could do for Ivy, Quinn's attention returned to herself. The ladder was gone now.
Even if the distance from the loft to the floor
hadn't been too great to jump, the floor below
her was ablaze.

She was trapped.

Waves of thick, gray smoke and searing heat
rose up to meet her, forcing her to back up into

a dark corner of the loft. Coughing, eyes watering, Quinn's frantic gaze searched the small, high platform for a way out. Wait . . . over there . . . off to her left . . . boards laid vertically instead of horizontally like the rest of the wood. A . . . small . . . door?

Crawling on her hands and knees, keeping one hand over her mouth and nose against the smoke and heat, Quinn moved slowly, carefully along the platform, until she reached the vertical boards.

It *was* a door . . . a small one, arched at the top. Probably used, a long time ago, to toss hay down from the loft.

How long ago? So long ago that the small rusted hinges, which Quinn could clearly see now, wouldn't open?

Waste of time. Very little time left. Hard to breathe, and so hot, so hot . . .

Instead of wrestling with the small black latch on the inside of the door, Quinn sat up and began kicking, kicking with all her might, her sneakered feet slamming against the door. Her chest hurt and tears from the smoke were pouring out of her eyes, and coughing wracked her upper body, but still she kicked, crying out, "Open, damn you, open!"

The door didn't open, but one particularly fierce blow splintered a board, enough to let in a whiff of fresh air. It felt so delicious that Quinn, gulping it in gratefully, kicked again with renewed strength. A second board splintered, and then gave way completely, leaving a hole the size of a shoebox.

But the flames were crackling viciously now, leaping up into the air, taunting Quinn with their hot breath.

Kicking, kicking . . . so tired, but mustn't stop now . . . another board and then another gave way. The hole had enlarged, its jagged edges forming a good-sized rectangle. Not big enough to squeeze through, but big enough to push her head through and fill her aching lungs with fresh air. And then to scream.

Quinn sat up, scuttled closer to the hole, thrust her head out, scratching one cheek on the ragged edge of a board, and crying out in pain.

The fire below her roared angrily.

When she had swallowed enough air to ease the pain in her chest, she opened her mouth to scream for help. The sound that came out was pitiful, a hoarse croak.

Tears of frustration joined the smoke-induced tears in Quinn's eyes. Help was so far away. How could anyone asleep in Nightingale Hall hear that pathetic little sound she'd just made? Her vocal chords must have been affected by the smoke.

Exhausted, terrified, her legs scalded by the intense heat directly beneath her, Quinn sagged against the little broken door, tempted to give up. Help . . . she needed help . . . she couldn't get out of this place alone.

Desperate, she raised her eyes heavenward. And saw the pulley.

A small, metal pulley, attached to the front of the barn. There was a thick rope wound around it. The tip of the rope dangled loosely, temptingly, over Quinn's head. She couldn't tell how long the rope was. But what did it matter if it didn't carry her all the way to the ground? It would at least get her out of this inferno.

At the same moment, a light went on upstairs in Nightingale Hall. Quinn knew no one had heard her cry for help. Had they heard the flames crackling?

Someone would be coming to help.

But she couldn't wait. There wasn't time.

She could probably squeeze her chest and arms through the jagged hole. But it wasn't large enough for her whole body. It would do her no good to grab the rope with her hand if she couldn't get the rest of her through the hole. She had to make the hole larger.

But there was no time . . .

She pulled her head backward, out of the hole. A lick of flame jumped up behind Quinn and caught a small pile of straw in its mouth, devouring it.

The hungry flame would be coming for her next.

With a hoarse, desperate roar, Quinn drew both legs backward and, using them as a battering ram, drove them straight into the wounded little door.

It fell open, dangling from its hinges like a broken-winged bird.

Instantly, Quinn jumped up, leaned out of the open space, one hand holding onto the wall for leverage, and stretched upward, straining until one hand touched the rough tip of the rope. Carefully, her fingers closed around it and pulled it toward her.

Another light went on in Nightingale Hall, then another. Over the roar of the flames, Quinn was vaguely aware of faint shouting. The shouting grew louder, came closer. Footsteps thudded down the slope in front of her. Startled cries and more shouting, near her now. A siren sounded faintly in the distance.

But as her hand closed around the rope, a crashing sound behind her brought her head around to look back into the barn. The rear half of the platform she was standing on had collapsed. There was only a dark hole where she had been sitting when Ivy came into the barn.

Ivy . . .

The siren sound moved closer . . . fire trucks, on their way to save her.

No time . . .

Clutching the end of the rope with both fists, Quinn took a deep breath, closed her eyes . . . and jumped.

Halfway down, she was brutally jerked to a standstill.

The rope was too short.

And flames were escaping from the building now, stabbing outward like snakes' tongues, straining outward to sear her, to consume her rope, and send her crashing to the ground.

She hung there, swaying above the hard ground, her face and arms feeling the hot breath of the fire.

"Jump!" someone shouted from below her. "Jump! You have to jump!"

She looked down. Below her, a group of people stood in a circle. They were all looking up at her. And they were holding something in their hands. It was stretched out across the circle, so that instead of seeing hard, dark ground, she saw white, as if that circle of ground had been covered with snow.

A sheet? A blanket?

They were holding a sheet or a blanket. Holding it up high, every person in the circle holding onto the edges for dear life.

For *her* dear life.

"Let go!" someone shouted. "Let go! We'll catch you!"

A hot stab of flame singed Quinn's elbow.

"Let go of the rope! Now!"

She let go.

And dropped, dropped, dropped, the heat from the burning building making her as dizzy as the fall itself.

She landed in the blanket, bounced once as if on a trampoline, and then lay still.

The fire truck screeched up the driveway.

Someone ran to direct the fire fighters.

"Ivy," Quinn said hoarsely as people helped her off the blanket. "Ivy Green is in there."

And by the way someone replied, "In *there*?" Quinn knew there was no hope. Not for Ivy.

But then . . . maybe there hadn't been any hope for Ivy in a long, long time.

While the fire fighters tackled the blaze, Quinn, the blanket wrapped around her shoulders, sat with Jess and Ian, wiping her face with a cool cloth Jess had brought her.

When the fire was out, when the fire truck had gone and the police had arrived, Quinn went inside Nightingale Hall to answer their questions. Jess and Ian stayed with her.

The first question the police officer asked her was, "May I ask you what you were doing in the barn, miss?"

Quinn, lying on a couch with the blanket over her, her cuts and bruises being tended to by Nightingale Hall's housemother, Mrs. Coates, wanted to say, "Well, officer, I can tell you this. I *wasn't* sleepwalking."

But she didn't. He wouldn't understand.

Instead, she told him everything that had happened that night.

Epilogue

The following morning. Quinn, her hands mittened in white gauze, lay in the narrow infirmary bed surrounded by her friends. Her head throbbed dully and her chest ached from smoke-tortured lungs, but for the first time in weeks, she felt completely, totally safe. Simon was sitting on the edge of her bed, holding one of her bandaged hands carefully in his, and Tobie and Suze stood on the opposite side.

She was safe.

But she still had questions.

"Suze," she asked hoarsely, "why did you tell me you were getting Reed's purse from the wrecked car? You weren't."

Suze's face flamed. "No, I wasn't," she said. And added sheepishly, "I had talked Jake into taking me for a ride in his car that afternoon. He didn't want to, but you know me . . . I just kept pushing until he gave in. We just went for a ride and came right back. When I got home, I didn't have my psych notebook, and I knew it had to be in his car. I figured the police would be returning all that stuff to Jake, and Reed knows what a barracuda I am when it comes to boys. I was afraid if she found that notebook, she'd think the worst. And it wasn't true. So, I knew I had to get that notebook back."

"Well, since it's confession time," Tobie said quietly, "I might as well tell you, Quinn, that I haven't been seeing Danny when you thought I was."

Quinn didn't admit that she already knew that. If Tobie had decided to talk, she wasn't going to interrupt.

"I like Danny," Tobie went on, "but I'm just not ready for another relationship. Not yet. I didn't think it was fair to be with Danny when I was thinking of Peter the whole time. But I didn't want to tell you, because I knew you thought it was good for me to get involved with someone." She looked directly at Quinn. "But I can't. Not yet. I'm working on it, and I think I'm doing better. The counselor has been a big help. I was with her almost all day yesterday. That's why you couldn't find me. She says I've got time, that I shouldn't rush it. And I think she's right."

"So do I," Quinn croaked.

"You do?"

"Sure. It sounds perfectly healthy to me. You're dealing with your feelings. Ivy didn't. She twisted them into something angry and ugly and then she turned that against other people. But . . ." Quinn smiled to take any sting out of her words, "no more secrets, okay?"

Tobie nodded. "No more secrets."

Quinn's eyes filled with tears then, thinking of Ivy. "It's so weird," she said softly, "in a way, it was a secret that was Ivy's undoing. The secret of my sleepwalking. But," she added lightly, "at least I know now I've only done it twice since I got to Salem. I thought for a while that I was doing it all the time, but it was just those two times when Tobie brought me back."

Suze cleared her throat. "Ah, I hate to break this to you, Quinn, but it was three times."

"Three?"

"Yeah. I brought you back once, too. The night Jake and Reed were attacked in their car. And that time, you weren't just out in the hall. I found you down in the lobby when I came home from my date that night. I couldn't believe it. There you were, in your sweats and a pair of white socks, looking like you had no idea where you were."

Quinn stared at her. "In the lobby? That night?"

"Right. I felt sorry for you, because you had these clean white socks on, and people had been tracking across the tile all night with wet, muddy feet. I knew your socks were going to get filthy. Anyway, I could tell you weren't awake, so I just turned you around and took you back to bed. You never said a word. When I told Tobie the next day, she explained that you do that sometimes. But I never said anything to you because I didn't want to embarrass you."

The socks. The socks that Meg had pointed out when they had all gathered in room 602 after the attack on the car. She really *had* been sleepwalking that night.

"Okay, okay," Quinn said, relieved to finally know the truth about that night. "Three times, then. But no more than that. And I have a feeling it's not going to happen again."

The nurse came in then, and ordered everyone out. "You can come back later, after she's rested. She needs her sleep."

Feeling safe, Quinn closed her eyes, certain for the first time in a long while that she wouldn't be setting one foot outside the bed until she was wide awake again.

She slept.

Sorority Sister

Omega Phi Delta.

Maxie ran her finger slowly over the letters on her new sorority sweatshirt.

She couldn't believe they'd actually pledged her. Out of all the girls who'd rushed Omega, she was one of the few — the lucky few — to be selected.

Everyone knew Omega Phi Delta was the best sorority on campus. Omegas were the coolest girls. They dated the most gorgeous guys and threw the wildest parties.

Becoming an Omega was like a dream come true for Maxie.

But the dream was about to become a nightmare.

Because something was terribly wrong at the Omega house.

Something deadly . . .

About the Author

"Writing tales of horror makes it hard to convince people that I'm a nice, gentle person," says **Diane Hoh**.

"So what's a nice woman like me doing scaring people?

"Discovering the fearful side of life: what makes the heart pound, the adrenalin flow, the breath catch in the throat. And hoping always that the reader is having a frightfully good time, too."

Diane Hoh grew up in Warren, Pennsylvania. Since then, she has lived in New York, Colorado, and North Carolina, before settling in Austin, Texas. "Reading and writing take up most of my life," says Hoh, "along with family, music, and gardening." Her other horror novels include *Funhouse*, *The Accident*, *The Invitation*, *The Fever*, and *The Train*.

WARNING Thrillers by **Diane Hoh** contain irresistible ingredients which may be hazardous to your peace of mind!

☐ BAP44330-5	**The Accident**	$3.25
☐ BAP45401-3	**The Fever**	$3.25
☐ BAP43050-5	**Funhouse**	$3.25
☐ BAP44904-4	**The Invitation**	$3.25
☐ BAP45640-7	**The Train**	$3.25

Available wherever you buy books, or use this order form.

THRILLERS

R.L. Stine

- ☐ MC44236-8 The Baby-sitter — $3.50
- ☐ MC44332-1 The Baby-sitter II — $3.50
- ☐ MC46099-4 The Baby-sitter III — $3.50
- ☐ MC45386-6 Beach House — $3.25
- ☐ MC43278-8 Beach Party — $3.50
- ☐ MC43125-0 Blind Date — $3.50
- ☐ MC43279-6 The Boyfriend — $3.50
- ☐ MC44333-X The Girlfriend — $3.50
- ☐ MC45385-8 Hit and Run — $3.25
- ☐ MC46100-1 The Hitchhiker — $3.50
- ☐ MC43280-X The Snowman — $3.50
- ☐ MC43139-0 Twisted — $3.50

Caroline B. Cooney

- ☐ MC44316-X The Cheerleader — $3.25
- ☐ MC41641-3 The Fire — $3.25
- ☐ MC43806-9 The Fog — $3.25
- ☐ MC45681-4 Freeze Tag — $3.25
- ☐ MC45402-1 The Perfume — $3.25
- ☐ MC44884-6 The Return of the Vampire — $2.95
- ☐ MC41640-5 The Snow — $3.25
- ☐ MC45682-2 The Vampire's Promise — $3.50

Diane Hoh

- ☐ MC44330-5 The Accident — $3.25
- ☐ MC45401-3 The Fever — $3.25
- ☐ MC43050-5 Funhouse — $3.25
- ☐ MC44904-4 The Invitation — $3.50
- ☐ MC45640-7 The Train — $3.25

Sinclair Smith

- ☐ MC45063-8 The Waitress — $2.95

Christopher Pike

- ☐ MC43014-9 Slumber Party — $3.50
- ☐ MC44256-2 Weekend — $3.50

A. Bates

- ☐ MC45829-9 The Dead Game — $3.25
- ☐ MC43291-5 Final Exam — $3.25
- ☐ MC44582-0 Mother's Helper — $3.50
- ☐ MC44238-4 Party Line — $3.25

D.E. Athkins

- ☐ MC45246-0 Mirror, Mirror — $3.25
- ☐ MC45349-1 The Ripper — $3.25
- ☐ MC44941-9 Sister Dearest — $2.95

Carol Ellis

- ☐ MC46411-6 Camp Fear — $3.25
- ☐ MC44768-8 My Secret Admirer — $3.25
- ☐ MC46044-7 The Stepdaughter — $3.25
- ☐ MC44916-8 The Window — $2.95

Richie Tankersley Cusick

- ☐ MC43115-3 April Fools — $3.25
- ☐ MC43203-6 The Lifeguard — $3.25
- ☐ MC43114-5 Teacher's Pet — $3.25
- ☐ MC44235-X Trick or Treat — $3.25

Lael Littke

- ☐ MC44237-6 Prom Dress — $3.25

Edited by T. Pines

- ☐ MC45256-8 Thirteen — $3.50